The Greatest Gift

Roxy Boroughs

Copyright 2015 Donna Ann Tunney
All rights reserved

Publisher: Baucis & Philemon
Editors: Linda Styles at Editing with Style
and Ted Williams, Freelance Editor
Cover: Kim Killion at Hot Damn Designs

No part of this book may be used or reproduced in any manner whatsoever without written permission, except in the case of brief quotations embodied in critical articles and reviews.

This is a work of fiction. Names, characters, places and incidents are the product of the author's imagination or are used fictitiously. Any resemblance to actual persons, living or dead, business establishments, events or locales is entirely coincidental.

ISBN-13: 978-1519615633
ISBN-10: 1519615639

For Barry,
my very own romance hero.

Thanks to C.J. Carmichael, B.C. Deeks, Pamela Yaye, Lecia
Cornwall and the Calgary Chapter of the
Romance Writers of America
for their suggestions and unwavering support.
Also, a big thank you to Dave Dixon
for his firefighting expertise.
Any errors in the execution are mine, not his.
A final thanks to Rachel Platten for her hit, *Fight Song*,
my theme music for this story.

CHAPTER ONE

Zack Jones jumped off the running board of Fire Truck 1 before the vehicle came to a complete stop. His heart sank as black smoke drifted from the building and flames spiked—bright and orange as a second sunset against the late November sky.

"There goes my paycheck," he muttered, as he masked up and secured his helmet.

Who'd have thought volunteering with the fire department in Carol Falls, Vermont, would bring him here? To Billy Boy's, where he worked as a full-time bouncer, filling in as bartender whenever Billy wanted time off.

Apparently, they'd both get vacations now. Unplanned ones. At best, the place would need repairs. At worse, it would end up in ashes along with a couple of his fellow firefighters.

Zack readied the thirty-pound hose, carrying it on his shoulder as he scanned the upper level. Mrs. Trivett lived in a small apartment above the bar. Not the most suitable spot for an elderly lady, but the rent was cheap due to the loud music. Which didn't bother Mrs. Trivett once she removed her hearing aids. She usually played euchre Wednesday nights, but a recent hip operation cramped her card-sharking fun.

He spied movement at the door to the fire escape and handed off the hose to another member of his team. Zack sprinted to the stairs—his hundred-pound protective gear weighing him down, adrenaline lifting him up.

As he hit the bottom step, he saw Mrs. Trivett above him, urged from the burning building by her grandson, Connor. The young man wore jeans and nothing else—no shirt, no shoes. The wind whipped red welts on Connor's thin chest, and sent the elderly woman's nightgown beating against her bare legs.

She eyed the drop to the ground below and froze.

Zack pounded up the stairs, reaching the pair as a window on the lower level shattered from the heat inside.

"I'll take her," Zack yelled to Connor through his mask.

He lifted Mrs. Trivett in his arms and carried her down the stairs, Connor sticking close.

Zack breathed a sigh of relief when he saw police cars blocking off the area. He also spotted several members of the Ladies' Auxiliary arriving on the scene. He recognized Sylvia Frost from her silvery-blond bob. She huddled in conference with his dark-haired mother, Diane, and Linda Boychuk, the sister-in-law of the building's owner.

Once Zack got his charges to safety, the ladies swarmed around Mrs. Trivett and her grandson, giving comfort in the form of blankets and hot beverages. That left Zack free to sidle up to the fire chief, Ian King, and hear their next move.

"Can't see in the building," Ian reported. "Smoke aside, there's a half inch of grime on the windows, and plastic Christmas wreaths, too—all blocking visibility." His green eyes locked on Zack. "You know the layout better than anyone. You lead."

Zack nodded and crouched low as he made his way through the entrance, his buddies clinging to the hose as they followed. The water they used to douse the structure bubbled to a boil at their feet.

Blinded by smoke and dripping with perspiration, Zack relied on memory and instinct to maneuver his way through the maze of tables and chairs. The heat and noise from the inferno grew as he approached the fire's source, his breathing apparatus making him sound like Darth Vader.

One more step and flames appeared, rolling up to the ceiling. He couldn't see the main counter for smoke. Couldn't see the wall in front of him. Or the photograph he knew hung there, of a smiling Billy, his staff and…one waitress in particular. A certain blonde, with the saddest smile Zack had ever come across.

He aimed the hose and made a pact with himself. He'd fight to save the bar and reclaim that photo, no matter the odds. The building provided a home to Mrs. Trivett and much-needed jobs in the town.

And the picture was the only shot he had of the one, unforgettable woman from his past.

Heather Connolly grabbed the railing and hauled herself up the next flight of stairs to her third floor apartment. After a double-shift juggling pints of beer, while balancing in high heels, she could barely feel her baby toes. Her insteps, however, were on fire.

Traipsing through the snowy parking lot had helped cool the pain, and the faulty heater in her car had kept the vehicle cold enough that she felt she'd driven home wearing icepacks on her feet. Thank goodness she'd switched to sneakers before hopping into her car.

As if.

There'd been no *actual* hopping involved at the end of this evening. Limping was more like it. At thirty-four, she was one of the older cocktail waitresses at the bar, and the wacky hours tired her. She felt the wear and tear on her knees—not to mention the hands on her derriere. The Hopportunist, Burlington's trendiest new bar, serviced an extremely tactile male clientele.

Heather chuckled. Even the place she worked had a *hop* in it.

And, in half a flight more, she'd be a *hop*, skip and a jump from her apartment. And the precious soul asleep in it.

There was no bitterness in her laugh now, only a sweet ache in her chest as her heart expanded—thankful she had another chance with her six-year-old daughter.

For Lottie, Heather would happily endure all the pinches and foot throbbing life had to offer. The job gave her a steady paycheck and good tips. She even liked the staff. Though she didn't feel the same sense of belonging she'd had in her last job, in the last town.

But she'd made a mistake there...hurt people...and could never go back.

A familiar tightness started in her throat and worked its way to her stomach. She freed her hair from its clip and let the long, blond strands fall, hiding her face from the world. True, the bad thing she'd done in Carol Falls was for Lottie, but that did little to ease the shame. Doing bad things for a good reason never ended well.

At least, not for Heather.

She yanked the fire door to the third floor, stepped through and gulped the stale hallway air. Ambrosia, after the climb.

While searching for her apartment key, she heard her phone beep. She pulled it from her purse, read the text message and frowned. It was from her sister, Fern. Another bid to take Lottie. This time, on a shopping trip to New York.

Over Christmas.

Fern meant well, attempting to give Lottie what Heather couldn't. Pretty dresses, a trendy new toy, maybe a front row seat to the latest Broadway musical. But there was no way Heather was going to endure a second Christmas without her daughter. Not when the two of them were so excited about spending the holidays together.

They'd already started on the decorations, creating a colorful wreath made of leftover bits of wrapping paper, and a life-size cardboard fireplace from which they'd hang the striped stockings Heather had knitted. They might live in a humble apartment, but it was theirs, and it was home. That made Heather richer than any Rockefeller or Onassis, regardless of her bank statement.

She jammed the phone into her purse, found her keys and unlocked her apartment door. Opening it, Heather was surprised to find her daughter dancing.

Dancing when she should have been in bed and asleep. Hours ago.

Lottie looked like a winter princess, dressed in a silver gown, her long blond hair trailing behind her. Sky blue makeup covered her forehead and cheekbones, with sparkly white snowflakes painted on top. Lottie's lashes glittered, too.

"Do you like my costume, Mommy? I'm a snowflake."

"I can see that. You look fabulous." Heather leaned down and embraced her daughter, while shooting her babysitters a questioning glance.

Lottie's grandmother, Ruth, stood at the ironing board pressing shiny, green material—her careworn face weighed down by shoulder length salt and pepper hair. Ruth's daughter, Wenda, a college-bound eighteen-year-old, was easily Lottie's favorite aunt. She sat on the second-hand couch, an array of makeup set out on the scarred coffee table in front of her.

"Another bad dream," Ruth whispered, responding to Heather's silent question.

So that's why Lottie was awake.

Again, Heather experienced that tightness. It was the third nightmare this week—far too many for a little girl to bear. And the reason why Heather always declined her sister's offers to take care of Lottie.

How could she explain Lottie's night terrors? Or her extreme shyness. Fern's hubby, a beefy golf enthusiast, and a reasonable guy normally, didn't understand why Lottie withdrew into herself every time he came near. At first, he'd tried to gain her affection with bribes of dolls and ice cream. When those tactics failed, he grew indifferent. A cool, six-foot-two iceman. The last thing Lottie needed. But tonight...

Tonight, Lottie was the smiling center of attention. She twirled on her tiptoes, glowing in the company of her regular sitters—the mother and younger sister of Heather's ex-husband. The handsome, charming, angry man who'd brought them all together.

Heather kicked off her sneakers, stuffed her gloves in her coat pocket, and chucked the lot in the hall closet, shutting the door on them. Along with her fears.

"Wenda and Grandma are putting on a play, Mommy. Can we go see it?"

"We're just helping with it," Ruth clarified, while Wenda muted the evening news program they'd been watching on the 20-inch TV—a hand-me-down from Heather's sister. "It's a spoken-word version of *The Nutcracker* for the Winter Recital. There's no ballet in the script at all. Though, a couple of the Belmont kids are doing a jazz number." She waved a hand, as if erasing the introduction of that side topic, and got back on track. "Rehearsals started in October, but they didn't call on us for help until now. It's going to be so exciting, and will give everyone something to do along with Frosty Frolics."

Remembering the latter event from the previous year, Heather's cheeks heated. Every December, the Frost family held the community celebration at their maple syrup farm in Carol Falls. There was singing, good food—even a visit from Santa.

If only she'd stayed away last year.

Lottie tugged on her arm. "Can we go to the play, Mommy? Please?"

Carol Falls was the last place Heather wanted to revisit. Maybe

Ruth and Wenda would take Lottie for a sleepover.

A good idea. If it weren't for those nightmares.

"Actually," Ruth began, "we were hoping Lottie could be *in* the play."

In it? "You said rehearsals started in October."

"Yes, for the adults and teens. They'd always planned to bring in some younger children, Lottie's age, to be snowflakes, mice and toy soldiers. They're small non-speaking parts, and don't require a lot of rehearsal. Also, they didn't want the young ones getting bored. Or overtired."

And Lottie never slept well.

If that weren't enough to squash the idea, the registration cost would. Community theaters generally charged a membership fee. Likewise, children's drama camps needed tuition money to run. Surely the organizers weren't relying on ticket sales to recoup their upfront expenses for sets and costumes.

About to decline, Heather caught her daughter's eye. The flicker of excitement in them turned to anxiety. Heather's own eyes watered as the girl then dropped her gaze in defeat, as if she already knew they couldn't afford it.

A six-year-old shouldn't be so wise. Or meek. Maybe a play would help build Lottie's confidence.

"I'm volunteering my services as a seamstress," Ruth continued. "But for Wenda, it's a paying gig and will look good on her résumé. Everyone else is donating their time, and several of the local businesses are acting as sponsors in return for a mention in the program. It's a real community affair."

Sounded like a golden opportunity for Wenda, who planned a career as a professional makeup artist—for stage, film and TV. Though, oddly, she rarely wore makeup herself. Mannishly dressed, the tall, artsy young woman reminded Heather of a train—with drive and determination to spare. Boxy attire squared-up Wenda's feminine curves and thick, black hair billowed from her head like smoke.

"They're really desperate for more little kids, even if they don't live in Carol Falls," Wenda added. "I asked if I could invite one of the children from my family, and they said that'd be great. They meet on weekends, and the first day for the young kids is next Sunday. The dress rehearsals and performance happen the week before Christmas."

As a child, Heather had enjoyed a couple of small roles in school plays. More than performing, she'd relished the sense of community, of being part of the group. Maybe Lottie would, too. But what about the repeated drives back and forth to Carol Falls?

She supposed Lottie might nap in the car. Or she could take the girl out of school early, rather than see her overtired. Lottie was bright and at the top of her class. An extra-long holiday might do her good, and give them some added time together after the trauma of last year's separation.

She ran her hand along Lottie's chin. "Would you like to be in the play, honey?"

Lottie's smile was all the 'yes' Heather needed. She'd vowed never to return to Carol Falls, but she wasn't going to let her child down. Somehow, she'd find a way to see Lottie's performance, without alerting anyone else in town to her presence. Maybe a scarf and dark glasses would do the trick. Heather rolled her eyes at her own dramatic thoughts.

"Can I be a snowflake in the play, Auntie Wenda? Can we both be snowflakes?"

Wenda slathered cleanser on Lottie's face. "Only little kids get to be snowflakes, but we can dress up together another time. Either as snowflakes, or...maybe we can go as Stan Laurel and Oliver Hardy." Wenda looked Heather's way and smirked. "I went out as Oliver for Halloween and none of the kids in my drama class had ever heard of him."

"Who's Olive Oil?" Lottie asked, gazing at her aunt with big, innocent eyes.

"Olive*r*," Wenda corrected. "Oliver Hardy. And it's okay that *you* don't know, because he made funny movies a long, long time ago—way before you were born. I found his photo in a book of old film stars. I'll bring it next time we get together." She wiped the remaining blue makeup from Lottie's face with a baby wipe. "Now, you go wash up properly, little snowflake."

Lottie scrunched her nose in protest.

"I'll help you as soon as I say good-bye to your grandmother and aunt," Heather promised. Apparently satisfied with that, Lottie gave both her sitters a kiss and a hug, and scampered to the bathroom down the hall.

Wenda packed her makeup kit, as Ruth folded her newly pressed material and slipped it into her sewing bag. Heather was sorry to see them go.

Under normal circumstances, she wouldn't want any reminders of her ex in her life. But Ruth and Wenda had been such a huge help, willing to drive the hour round-trip from Carol Falls to Burlington to babysit whenever needed.

That's more than Heather's own parents were prepared to do. When she'd married and had a baby before her older sister—heaven forbid!—good ol' Mom and Dad had rejected Heather for upsetting their outdated notions about the timing of such things. Perhaps they'd lighten up once Fern produced a 'valid' grandchild.

Until that time, Heather would concentrate on her own kid, and associate with only the people who truly loved her little girl. She accompanied her guests to the door and retrieved their coats. "Thanks again for looking after Lottie."

"It's our pleasure," Ruth replied, wrapping a knitted scarf around her neck. "I'm grateful you allow us to spend time with her…especially after what happened between you and Chase."

The older woman croaked out the last few words, then turned away. Heather choked up, too. They'd both loved Chase. Both been betrayed by him.

"I'll see you tomorrow then," Heather sang out, to lighten the mood.

"Tomorrow it is," Ruth agreed.

Heather thanked them again, closed the apartment door and locked it. She gave herself a moment to put away the ironing board and don her game face. Sad eyes were the last thing Lottie needed to see, so Heather practiced a smile as she made her way through the living room, turning off lights as she went.

She reached for the TV remote, her finger poised over the red OFF button, and looked up in time to catch the headline across the bottom of the screen: BAR FIRE IN CAROL FALLS.

Pictured above was the place where she used to work, smoke rising past its blinking Christmas lights and curling into the night sky. Heather sank to the couch and turned up the volume.

"…Billy Boy's earlier this evening," the male announcer said, caught in mid-sentence. "The volunteer firefighters of Carol Falls, with assistance from the department in neighboring Waterbury, extinguished the blaze, preventing extensive damage. Zack Jones proved himself a hero—saving two tenants, one elderly, who lived in the second-floor apartment." A picture of Zack, wearing his bulky uniform, flashed on the screen.

Heather felt a flutter in her chest—part worry that he'd volunteered for such a dangerous job. Part...something else. Even with soot and sweat staining his face, the man looked mighty fine. Dark hair curled over his forehead. Warm, brown eyes gazed out at her like pools of rich chocolate. And his mouth...

That mouth left her breathless as she remembered how he'd caressed her with it on the one incredible night she'd spent in his bed.

They'd started as friends and ended as lovers. Until it *all* ended that evening.

Story over, the newscaster switched to the weather report, droning on about a winter storm on its way, while Heather remained on the couch, transfixed.

So, Zack Jones was the hero of Carol Falls. No surprise there. The guy definitely had the right goods—killer smile, loyal to a fault, and a six-pack that made Gerard Butler's warrior king, Leonidas, look like a wuss. All these things Heather knew firsthand.

Because, for a time, she'd fooled herself into believing Zack could be her hero, too.

CHAPTER TWO

The afternoon following the fire, Zack roamed through the wreckage, his boots chomping up the glass and wet debris littering the floor. The smell of burnt wood, both sweet and bitter, pressed hard against his chest.

Or maybe that crushing feeling came from seeing this old friend of a building lying wounded—black and bruised. Only yesterday people had been at Billy Boy's, eating greasy fries and drinking beer. Now, a layer of soot covered everything—the floor, the chairs, even the pool tables.

He stuffed his gloved hands into the pockets of his coat. They were lucky it was winter. The windows, which had been shut tight, kept out added oxygen that would have fed the fire and made things worse.

A whole lot worse.

Still, it wouldn't be a good Christmas for Billy, the owner of the bar. Or his staff.

Beside Zack, Ian gazed up at the charred rafters above the main counter and let out a sigh, his breath a puff of frosty white smoke in the air. "Hope you've got some money saved up. 'Cause you sure won't be earning any here for a while."

Zack nodded. No paycheck from anywhere, in fact. Although some fire departments gave their volunteers a small hourly rate to offset lost time at their real job, the volunteers at Carol Falls didn't receive a dime. Giving back to the community was their payment, and that had always been enough for Zack.

As fire chief, Ian King had the only paid position. And today proved why. It was his responsibility to determine the cause of the blaze and then generate an inch-thick report of his findings. Much like writing a high school essay, to Zack's way of thinking. Ian was welcome to the job.

As per his training, the boss always assumed the fire was deliberately set, checking into every possible cause in order to rule out foul play. If the blaze stumped him, or if he suspected arson, he could call for assistance to deal with the investigation. Today, he had an extra hand in Zack.

"Thanks for letting me tag along."

"Happy for the help, Schwartz," Ian replied, addressing Zack by his nickname. All the firefighters had one, even Ian. His was Axe, because no one could break down a door like he could. Zack's own moniker embarrassed him, which is probably why it stuck. The guys couldn't resist comparing him to a former Mr. Universe, who wound up as the *Governator* of California.

"Besides—" the chief continued as he made a note on the clipboard he carried "—you're familiar with the place. You'll be able to spot anything suspicious faster than me."

They'd started their investigation at the perimeter of the building—from the least to the most damaged area. That led them inside.

"I see there's a security camera in the far corner. We can check the footage and—"

"The camera's for show. Billy had it hooked up at one time, but the equipment broke down and he never repaired it. Figures the hardware is enough to scare folks into using their best behavior."

Ian scowled. "Please, tell me he had working smoke detectors."

"I check them, myself. Twice a year. Whenever we change the clocks to Daylight Savings Time, and back again."

"Good work."

Good, too, that Connor heard the alarm. If the young man hadn't been staying with his grandmother, Mrs. Trivett might not have realized the danger until it was too late.

Resuming the search, Zack scanned the large main room, taking in that familiar photo on the wall before looking at the scorched counter in front of it.

An uneasy chill skittered over the base of his neck, one that had nothing to do with the temperature. There was something on the bar that didn't belong—the remains of a lamp, its plastic base melted and the bulb in it shattered from the heat.

He pointed to it. "I've never seen this on the counter before."

"You think it started the fire?"

Zack spotted the charred remnants of newspapers nearby. "If someone used a bulb with a really high wattage—way over what's recommended—and put paper on top of the shade to ignite…"

Ian snapped a photo of the scene. "Think it was the owner?"

Zack shrugged. He'd known Billy Boychuk for years. A decade, at least. Billy had been a good boss. Given Zack a job when he needed it. Was it possible the man set fire to his own building?

Zack didn't want to believe it, but he couldn't rule out the possibility. Not without proof to the contrary. "If so, Billy wouldn't be the first guy to torch his place for the insurance money."

At that moment, as if on cue, the building's namesake, Billy Boychuk, entered with his brother in tow. Peter was as different from Billy as he was similar. Both were in their thirties and had a certain family resemblance—sandy hair, gray eyes, cleft chin. But Peter was slightly older, leaner and better groomed than the heavyset Billy, who lived in a perpetual rumple. Peter was also married with a couple of kids, where Billy remained a childless bachelor.

Ian stepped forward and held out his arms to block the duo. "Hey, fellas. I have to ask you to stay put until we finish our investigation."

Billy jerked to a stop and Peter almost bumped into him. "Yeah. Sure thing. Sorry. Just wanted to know how long you'll be. I need to get Jim Frost in here to see what he can do."

Frost was the second son of one of the original Carol Falls families and a cousin of Ian's on his mother's side. Jim had moved back to town last Christmas and set himself up as a local contractor. The best in the area.

"If the building can be saved, Jim's the man to do it," Ian agreed.

"Speaking of saved, thanks for getting Mrs. Trivett out safe."

Zack gave a quick nod of acknowledgement, keeping his eye on the speaker. Certainly, Billy's demeanor didn't reveal any signs of guilt. His brow puckered with concern and the bags under his eyes betrayed a lack of sleep, but Billy's color was good, and his voice held steady as his gaze swept over the ruin before him.

Then again, maybe the guy was an ace at poker.

Peter undid the top button of his smart, wool coat. "I thought Mrs. Trivett played bridge on Wednesdays."

"She recently had a hip replacement," Zack told him. "Didn't feel like going out this week. That's why her grandson's here. To give her a hand."

"Well, we'll let you two get at it." Billy turned to leave, then did an about-face. "There's something else I came for…"

"The deposit?" Zack suggested. Mostly because he wanted his pay, and he knew his fellow staffers would need the pre-Christmas cash, too.

Billy snapped his fingers. "Right." He stepped forward and, again, Ian blocked him.

"I'll open the safe for you," Zack offered, playing referee.

Almost everyone on staff knew the combination. They often had to get change for the cash register or, on a busy night, they'd stash extra money in it. Best not to have too much accessible, in case some punk decided to pull a robbery. A sad reality at this time of year. Christmas made some people do desperate things.

Zack maneuvered his way to the other side of the counter and squatted in front of the safe. He removed one glove, punched in the nine-digit number, cranked open the door, and sucked in a breath. "You sure you didn't make the deposit already, Billy?"

"No. I planned to do it this afternoon. Thursday. Like always. Why?"

Zack pulled back the heavy door so everyone could see. "Because the safe is empty."

Peter's face dropped. "Tell me you're joking."

"I wouldn't kid about that."

The accountant turned to his brother. "When was the last time you changed the combination?"

"It's been so long," Billy began, rubbing his forehead. "I can't remember."

"Isn't that the point of having a digital lock?" Peter asked. "That way you can change it whenever one of your staff leaves."

His brother bristled. "I've got enough numbers running through my head without having debit PINs and safe combinations clogging it up. Besides, most of my people have been with me for years."

Zack knew of at least one person who'd quit and moved on—the blond woman in the photo.

He shoved that fact to the back of his mind as Ian punched in 9-1-1 on his cell phone. The cheery electronic melody broke through the shocked silence.

This was a matter for the police…because their fire had turned into arson.

To hide a burglary.

Heather reached the fire door on her floor, after another double shift—her legs as stiff and sore as if she'd run a marathon. The first week of December had blown in, bringing office parties to The Hopportunist, along with a winter flu that left them short-staffed.

Then police officers had appeared. To question *her!*

Just a formality, they'd said. They were interviewing all of Billy Boy's employees—past and present. "When were you last in Carol Falls?" they'd asked. "Do you know anyone who'd want to steal from Billy?"

The presence of the 'uniforms' had sent half of tonight's staff into a nervous frenzy. Plates and glasses slipped off trays and crashed to the floor to shouts of, "Opa!" The other half of the staff—the *female* half—eyed the handsome male officer and whispered about the possibilities of him posing for one of those police calendars.

Too much excitement for Heather, by far.

She forced exhaustion to one side, knowing she had the morning free before going back to work the following evening. With Lottie at school, she could pay some bills. Maybe indulge in more window shopping for gifts.

She hadn't quite decided what to get Lottie for Christmas—apart from the hat, scarf and mitts set she'd knitted. Clothes were practical, but she wanted to make this year really special. Though she could use the extra pay, she'd already booked Christmas Eve off to spend it with her daughter.

Behind the door of her apartment, she heard a male voice coming from inside. Probably, Ruth and Wenda watching the news again. Heather could only hope her baby was sleeping peacefully this time.

Heather pulled out her key, twisted it in the lock and opened the door. Two police officers stood in her living room. On the couch, Wenda cradled a red-eyed Lottie.

Ruth rushed to meet Heather. "We tried explaining to these officers that there's been a horrible mistake. They were here earlier and took a look around. I didn't see any harm in it. But this? This is outrageous."

The male officer approached—the good-looking one from earlier tonight. "Heather Lynn Connolly?"

"Yes?"

"We have a warrant for your arrest."

She must have misheard. "I know I didn't go over the speed limit on the way home. The roads are too icy and—"

"You're under arrest for the burglary and arson at Billy Boy's Pool Hall in Carol Falls," the same officer said, showing her the warrant, while his female associate revealed a pair of handcuffs.

Heather tucked her arms into her chest and locked them there. "I didn't do it. I'm innocent."

"That'll be for the courts to decide, ma'am." The male officer—who didn't look so handsome now—then read her Miranda rights, raising his voice to be heard over Lottie's whimpers.

"Mommy...Mommy...Mommy..."

A tremor went through Heather. Her body started to shake. This couldn't be happening—a nightmarish repeat of last year's police visit. Officers had come to the door to make an arrest then, too. Only then, *Chase* had been the one to go to jail.

She tried to get to her daughter, but the male officer barred her way. "Please...let me go to her."

"Best you come with us now, ma'am."

"I will. But I need to talk to my daughter first. *Please.*"

The officers exchanged a look. Finally, the female spoke. "You've got one minute. Stay where we can see you."

Heather ran to Lottie and hugged her tight. "Mommy? What's going on?"

"There's been a mistake, sweetheart. I have to go with the officers and clear everything up. But I'll be back, soon. I promise." Heather switched her gaze to Ruth. "Can she stay with you, while I straighten this out?"

"Of course."

Heather didn't trust her voice, so she nodded her thanks. She handed her child back to Wenda. "Can you please take Lottie to her room? I don't want her to see—"

Wenda tore down the hall with Lottie looking over her shoulder. The little girl's arms reached out, her mouth open wide in a silent scream. Heather jammed a fist between her teeth to hold in her own sobs.

"Hands behind your back."

Cuffs encased her wrists.

"Spread your feet," the female ordered, and gave Heather's left foot a rough nudge to make sure she complied. "Do you have any weapons on you? Anything that'll poke, prick, stick or cut me?"

"No. Nothing."

The woman searched Heather—checking coat pockets, patting her chest, her arms and legs. And she'd thought pinches at the bar were humiliating.

The officers led her from the apartment, one on each arm. Without their support, Heather feared she'd fall over.

How, in God's name, had she wound up like this? Accused of burning the same building Zack had risked his life to save.

CHAPTER THREE

Heather sat in a holding cell in the basement of the Carol Falls Court House. She'd spent the night on a thin mattress, staring at the scuffed, gray walls. Too worried to sleep, too shocked to cry.

She'd used her one phone call to reach out to the only lawyer she knew—her divorce attorney. He'd promised to contact a local colleague with the skills to help her.

She'd explained, to anyone who would listen, that the closest she'd come to Billy Boy's in the past year was watching the blaze on the evening news.

How long would it take the police to admit they had the wrong person in custody?

How long before she saw Lottie again?

Heather's night away from her daughter dragged on through to the next morning, anxiety filling each second. The last couple of Christmases had been tough on the little girl. First, police carted her daddy away for domestic violence, while an ambulance rushed Heather to the hospital. As a result, Lottie wound up with family services.

Thankfully, Fern had stepped in quickly and taken Lottie until Heather made a clean break from Chase. Once Heather could prove she'd created a safe, stable environment for her child on her own, with a fresh start in Burlington, Lottie was returned to her.

And now, for Lottie to see her second parent arrested...

Heather shivered, feeling cold—mostly inside. Without her coat, confiscated along with her purse, she could do little to keep warm except drape the cell's lone thin blanket over her shoulders and hug her chilled arms close to her body. Didn't the mayor's budget include heat for this place? The walk-in fridge at work was cozier.

Maybe the police kept it like this on purpose. To keep the prisoners in line.

Down the hall, a steel door opened and closed. Footsteps followed.

Since Heather was alone in the holding cells, she assumed the visitor was for her. Maybe her new lawyer.

She stood and smoothed her wrinkled clothes. The arresting officers hadn't let her change, so she was still in her cocktail dress from work—short, black, tight. Combined with her trusty sneakers, the outfit wasn't one to project the image of a steady, law-abiding citizen. They'd made her remove her laces, too, so the shoes slipped whenever she paced.

By the time Heather had finger-combed her hair, a young woman appeared from around the corner. She wore a brown corduroy dress that enveloped her body from neck to ankle. Long, thick hair overwhelmed the woman's features, which were further concealed by a pair of oversized glasses. She produced a paper bag and handed it to Heather through the bars.

"Thought you might like some breakfast."

"Thanks."

Heather took the bag and found a muffin inside, warm and packed with cranberries. The smell of it made her stomach churn—worry overriding hunger. She forced herself to take a bite and swallow.

"Are you my lawyer?"

"No. I'm the police dispatcher. My name's Taylor. Taylor Pope."

Now that Heather had a good look, she remembered seeing the woman in town a few times last year, but they'd never actually met.

Taylor came closer and lowered her voice. "You'll be facing the judge soon. I know you'll want to look your best." She reached into a pocket of her voluminous dress and pulled out a tube of lipstick. "I guessed at the color."

"You guessed well. I have this shade at home." Heather was about to slather some over her lips when Taylor produced a small, round mirror.

"I'd better hold it for you."

No doubt prisoners weren't allowed to have anything that could be used as a weapon. Mirrors could break and leave sharp edges.

Her new pal held the mirror up on her side of the bars. Heather bent at the knees to get a good view of the lower part of her face and smoothed on the lipstick.

"I brought some tissue, too. In case your mascara strayed."

Heather worked hard to scare up some saliva. She spit on the tissue and mopped at the dark bits under her eyes.

"I should take the lipstick. I'll put it with your other personal things."

"Thanks," Heather said, handing the tube back to Taylor. "This is really kind of you."

"People judge on appearances."

An odd thing for Taylor to say, since the muffin-bearing dispatcher did little to help her own looks. Yet she'd picked the perfect shade of lip color.

Before Heather could contemplate the incongruity, the steel door down the hall banged again.

"It's time." Though Taylor said the words gently, they still sounded ominous.

A policeman appeared—blond, blue-eyed and built. Heather had *definitely* seen this guy around town—Officer Erik Wedge. Even Taylor snuck a peek at him through her lashes.

Wedge maintained a stony expression, but when his eyes met Heather's she caught the flicker of recognition there. He remembered her, too. She bowed her head to avoid seeing the disappointment that was sure to follow.

He fitted Heather with handcuffs and led her out of the cell, down the hall and into a waiting elevator, where they rode in silence to the main floor of the town hall. Once there, Wedge escorted her to the courtroom and cuffed her to a chair in the empty jury box.

She heard the rustle of spectators, felt their gaze, but didn't return it—wasn't sure she'd survive the shame. Instead, she focused on the judge, clad in his coal-black robe.

Coal at Christmas. Coal in your stocking when you've been bad.

The clerk called her name. A dark-haired man, in a gray suit, stepped forward and spoke to the judge. From their exchange,

Heather learned her request for a court-appointed attorney had been approved.

"Do you need a minute to confer with your client?"

"Yes, Your Honor."

While the judge went on with the next case, the lawyer picked up a file from the clerk, headed over to the jury box and took a seat beside her.

"I'm Spencer Frost, your attorney," he said, in a half-whisper. "Please, call me Spence."

Good Lord—a Frost was representing her. She'd definitely landed in Hell.

"Do you understand the charges against you?"

"Arson and robbery."

"Burglary, actually—since no one was confronted during the alleged crime. As they would be in a holdup at a convenience store, for example."

Heather gazed at the pitcher of water by the judge with envy, her throat so dry she could hardly swallow. "How can I be accused of something I didn't do?"

"Apparently, Mayor Lincoln piled on the pressure for a fast arrest in the case. There may have been a rush to judgment. However, an eyewitness claims you set the fire. Based on that, the police had reason to suspect you of second-degree arson. *Second-degree* because people were in the building at the time. People who could have died. After all the terrorist scares, the authorities take public safety seriously.

"The officers said there were witnesses, but didn't tell me who."

"Connor Trivett is one. He's been staying with his grandmother in the apartment above Billy Boy's. The night of the fire, he went out for a cigarette. Saw a tall, blond woman enter the bar after closing. Thinking it unusual, he poked around and noticed a large, gold hoop earring on the ground near the entrance."

Her signature look. She used to wear a pair of hooped earrings all the time—even to bed. Until she lost one.

She'd tried to find a replacement, but the design was unusual, with a twisting band of rose gold. A graduation gift from her parents, before she disappointed them. She'd always hoped to find the missing earring. But not like this.

"Connor claims he observed you enter the building on the night in question. About twenty minutes later, he saw you run out...right before the smoke detector went off. He identified your picture and his grandmother, Mrs. Trivett, concurred that you were at Billy's that night."

"What picture?"

"Apparently, there's one of you behind the bar. Wearing the jewelry."

A year-old photo, taken after Chase smashed her jaw. She'd lost weight since. A diet of milkshakes, sipped through a straw, had puffed her up then. Not to mention the swelling in her face.

"I look different now."

"Not enough to confuse Connor. He picked your current mugshot from a photo line-up without hesitation. And the police found the matching earring in your jewelry box. Connor also described your car and knew the last three digits of your licence plate."

Heather winced. "The officers told me all about the 'so-called' evidence on the drive here."

"Yet, in your original interview, you said you hadn't been to Carol Falls for a year. I might be able to get around the car sighting. It was evening...and Connor didn't catch the full licence plate. But how do you explain the earring?"

"I can't. But the witnesses are wrong. They've mistaken me for someone else. I was at work the night of the fire. Miles away, in Burlington."

"Your boss vouched for you. But he also said you took all your breaks together that night."

So she could go window shopping for Lottie's Christmas present.

Heather added up the time in her head. Certainly enough for her to have raced from Burlington to Carol Falls, set the fire, then tear back to her job.

She replayed her steps that night. Could anyone else testify as to her whereabouts at the time? A store clerk, perhaps?

No. She hadn't talked to anyone. Merely roamed among the other shoppers, searching for that perfect gift.

Spence pushed a wayward curl from his forehead and leaned in, his blue eyes sharp. "Billy Boychuk said you left in a hurry last December. Never came in for your scheduled shift. Worried, he checked with your landlord here, and learned you'd broken your lease and disappeared. To the police, it appears you were upset with Billy. That maybe you were angry about something and wanted revenge."

Had the world gone crazy?

"That's ridiculous. Billy was good to me. I..."

How much could she tell Spence without making herself look worse? Heather took a deep, calming breath, while she selected her words.

"I had to leave town. I didn't have time to explain. Plus, if I were going to get back at Billy for something, why would I wait a whole year to do it?"

"Maybe so no one would suspect you." Spence looked down at his file and flipped through a couple of pages. "Billy told the police you never returned your key for the pub. Investigators found it in your jewelry box...next to the earring."

"Billy told me to keep the key, in case he was ever in a bind and needed me to open or lock up."

He'd said it when she'd called to ask if he wanted her to pop the key in the mail. She'd told him the chances of her going back to Carol Falls were pretty much non-existent, but he'd insisted she keep it. Told her she was a valued employee and that he hoped to win her back one day. She should have gone ahead and mailed the key to him but, at the time, she was happy to save the postage. *Stupid.*

She hadn't thought about the key in months. No doubt, Billy hadn't either. Having it in her possession sure made her look bad now, though.

"I understand there's a lot of incriminating evidence against me, but I did not steal money or set fire to the bar, Spence."

"So you want to plead innocent?"

"I *am* innocent."

"Good to hear. I prefer defending innocent clients." He gave her a smile, then sobered. "I did some research before meeting you. Every year, there are stories of people wrongfully imprisoned due to mistaken identity."

Heather could hardly believe it. Others found themselves trapped in the same predicament? "You think someone who looks like me could have committed the crimes?"

Spence rubbed his chin. "Possibly. Though one of your accusers, Mrs. Trivett, is a well-loved, upstanding citizen in the community. We won't score any points trying to discredit her."

Heather's optimism took a dive. She knew Mrs. Trivett's reputation. They'd have more luck smearing Betty White.

"Is my trial today?"

"No, this is your arraignment. You'll hear the formal charges against you. It's a slow morning for the judge, so he may entertain bail arguments, as well."

"How much will it be?"

"The judge will set a bail amount based on the severity of the crimes you're facing. As well as your flight risk."

Arson? Burglary? Heather imagined the courts wouldn't take those crimes lightly. And she'd run from Carol Falls last Christmas.

"I don't have much money. I had to start all over last year." While digging herself out of a pile of inherited debt.

"Any relatives you can call? A husband? Parents?"

"Not them. Maybe my sister…." No. She couldn't ask Fern. It wouldn't be right. "What happens if I don't make bail?"

"Until we resolve this, you'll be in custody."

"In jail?" A bead of sweat meandered down her back. "Those other people who were falsely accused, how long were they incarcerated before they got justice?"

"A month. Some longer."

Heather clutched the sleeve of his elegant suit jacket. "I've got to get out of here. I have a six-year-old daughter—"

"Good to know. The judge will take into consideration your ties to family, work and the community in determining your flight risk." Spence patted her hand. "It's okay. 'The best way out is always through…'"

She recognized the Robert Frost quote. Heather hoped the poet was right, because it would take all the courage she could muster to get through this ordeal.

The court clerk called her name and case number again, which prompted the judge to ask Spence, "Are we ready to proceed?"

"We are, Your Honor."

After Wedge reappeared and unshackled her, he led her to a chair at the defense table—the spot Chase occupied the last time she was in court.

"I'm going to do everything I can to help you," Spence told Heather. "Let me do all the talking."

No problem there. She was in such a state she could hardly breathe, let alone speak. And too nervous to take in much of the proceedings. But through the mist of her fears she heard the judge say one thing, loud and clear—the amount of her bail. Her heart stopped and her ears buzzed. She gripped the table to stand.

"I have a young daughter who needs me!"

The judge banged his gavel and Spence gestured for her to resume her seat. She fell into her chair and closed her eyes, praying she wouldn't faint.

Spence negotiated with the judge, arriving at a lower bail amount, but it was still a whole pile of money she didn't have. Then, to avoid the upcoming holidays, the judge scheduled her trial for January—on the day before Lottie turned seven.

A rustle in the courtroom told her the hearing was at an end, but not before the magistrate cautioned her: "Don't leave the State of Vermont."

A hand clasped her arm. She expected Officer Wedge with his steel cuffs but, instead, turned to find Fern.

Heather hugged her sister over the wooden railing that separated the court participants from the spectators. She hung on to the thin woman as if she were a buoy, sent to save her from drowning.

A second later, the officer read the riot act. "No touching. Hands where I can see them."

Heather stepped away from her sister, feeling as if a huge, cold gulf separated them.

"You came."

"Of course," Fern replied, her voice smoky from a former two-pack-a-day habit.

"How did you know?"

"It's all over the news, Sis."

Heather cringed. What would her boss think? Her landlord? The teachers and parents at Lottie's school?

"Where's Lottie?" Fern asked, reading her thoughts. "I can care for her, until you're free."

"Thanks. I really appreciate it. But Lottie is fine. Ruth has her."

Fern's mouth tightened. "You trust your mother-in-law? After what her son did to you?"

Heather shot a look at Spence and Wedge. She lowered her voice, hoping Fern would follow suit. "It's not Ruth's fault that Chase turned out the way he did. He broke her heart, too."

"Really?"

"Really." Heather suspected Chase took after his dad. She'd never met the man and knew only a few things about him—he liked his beer, and Chase had feared him. Unable to accept Ruth's second 'surprise' pregnancy, the senior Mr. Connolly threw a fit and ran off to Mexico with a younger woman. Not exactly the best choice in a partner if he wanted to avoid parenthood.

"They're a weird family."

By weird, Fern meant artsy. She mistrusted anyone who didn't make their money with numbers. Fern and her husband worked on Wall Street, the Numbers' Capital.

"Lottie's okay where she is."

"If you change your mind, you know I'm here for you." Fern fiddled with her purse, adjusting the strap. "In the meantime, we need to talk about your bail. I have some money saved up for another…well, never mind. You need it. It's yours."

Heather almost flung her arms around Fern again. She knew exactly what her sister had saved for. That Fern would willingly part with the money meant the world to Heather. "Thank you."

"At least, it's a start. Maybe you can go to a bondsman for the rest," Fern suggested. "I can't dip into our assets. Doug would have a fit."

Heather could imagine. And, although Fern's offer was incredibly generous, it was a Band-Aid solution, at best.

"I don't have anything to use as collateral for a bondsman." Her chances of spending Christmas with her daughter were melting away like snow during the spring thaw.

"I do," said a new voice. A man's. One she'd know anywhere.

Her heart hitched. She swiveled around and there stood Zack Jones, as gorgeous as she remembered—a deep wine-colored dress shirt stretched across his broad chest, a black tie at his throat. With his equally black, quilted jacket thrown over one shoulder, he stood ready and willing to rescue her. Her own, modern-day caped crusader.

But was the hero of Carol Falls really willing to back a

suspected felon?

Now that Zack had everyone's attention, he wasn't sure what to do with it.

He'd heard the buzz about Heather's arrest and court appearance. Who hadn't? There were few secrets in a small town.

He should have done himself a favor and stayed away. But he'd had to see her again.

Only he hadn't counted on witnessing the defeat on her face, the heartbreak over the separation from her child. When she'd stood and shouted that she had a daughter, he felt he'd taken a blow to the gut.

He wanted to help. Make her problems disappear. But how?

He could put up his house. It still carried a mortgage, but he had a lot of equity in it. Was he prepared to do that? After Heather had run off on him last Christmas?

"I've got some money saved." Yeah, funds that were supposed to see him through Billy Boy's closure. "If your sister's willing to go in with me, I'm sure we can get a bondsman to give us the rest."

For a moment, Heather looked at him with wide, watery eyes. Then she reached over the barrier separating them and wrapped her arms around him in a bear hug, Wedge hollering protests all the while.

Zack could hardly make out what Erik said, not with Heather's curves pressed against his body, her ragged breath warm against his neck, her cheek as soft against his as the mohair sweater she wore on their one amazing night together.

He embraced Heather with one arm, half-heartedly. If he really gave into the hug, he feared Erik would have an aneurism. While Zack, himself, wouldn't ever want to let her go.

He had to remember this was the woman who'd run out on him. She'd freed herself from a terrible marriage by then. Nothing held them back from a life together. And nothing held her back in his bed that night. He could still remember her kisses, the way she gave herself to him completely.

Damn, he'd almost proposed.

When he'd reached across his bed the next morning, the sheets were cold, her clothes were gone, and so was she. He found a hasty note tossed on his kitchen counter near the coffee maker. 'Thanks for everything, Zack. But I can't stay.'

Thanks for *everything?* Was that all their night together meant to her?

He backed away from their hug.

Spencer had argued that Heather wasn't a flight risk, but Zack knew better. And he worried that helping her now, was going to be the biggest mistake of his life.

Correction: the *second* biggest mistake. Falling for her last year had been the first.

CHAPTER FOUR

Zack put up his share of the bail money, alongside Fern.

Wren would have been a better name for Heather's sister, given her conservative brown suit and birdlike movements. When she opened her wallet, Zack marveled at the amount of plastic feathering the leather slots—membership cards, discount cards and credit cards—all neatly organized. Fern hardly glanced at the contents, as her quick fingers plucked out ID.

Bird stuff aside, she resembled Heather enough that you could tell they came from the same family—both tall, blond and pretty. Fern was more angular, though. Zack figured she didn't have to exercise to stay thin. She probably burned off calories alphabetizing her recycling.

They made small talk while they waited for Heather's release. Mostly chitchat about the weather. Yes, it was sunny. Yes, they'd probably have a white Christmas. Yes, Mexico was looking good right now. Zack almost did the happy dance when Heather finally appeared.

As the sisters hugged, he remembered the way Heather had wrapped her arms around him in the courtroom. That closeness stirred up feelings he didn't need. Or want.

Emotions confused things. Got you in trouble. And it was definitely over between them.

But, having been raised by a single mom, he could imagine what it must be like for Heather's little girl right now—separated from her only parent. So here he was, playing the Good Samaritan.

Zack had only one interest in Heather—recouping his part of the bail money. He planned to keep his heart at a distance, while sticking to her like glue.

"Want a ride back to Burlington?" Fern had told him Heather had made that city her home.

"Thanks, Zack. But I need to get to my mother-in-law's house, so I can see my little girl."

"No problem." He cupped her elbow and led her toward the exit, before Fern could offer to chauffeur. He wasn't about to let Heather out of his sight.

"I'll follow in my car," Fern said. "What are you driving, Zack?"

"A red Silverado." At her blank stare, he added, "A truck. You?"

"Toyota Corolla. A light tan color."

No surprise there.

He escorted the ladies out of the building, noting where Fern had parked. From their earlier exchange, he assumed she was looking for him to lead the way. Once Heather took her place in the passenger seat of his truck, he pulled out and waited at the exit of the parking lot, until he spotted Fern's car in his rear view mirror.

Following Heather's instructions, he headed away from the downtown area—warm air flowing out of the truck's heaters, his favorite country station filling the silence. They rode three blocks before Heather spoke again.

"Fern could have driven me."

"She seems nice."

"Yes. Yes, she is."

Another long pause while, on the radio, Patsy Cline fell to pieces.

In the old days, he'd felt comfortable around Heather. They could talk about anything. It was one of the qualities that originally drew Zack to her. After a shift at the bar, they'd sit together while she cashed out, and discuss all kinds of topics—politics, movies, music, football. He'd never met a woman who knew so much about sports.

"Fern and I haven't always gotten along," she went on, finally. "Our parents played us off each other—favoring one to make the other compliant. It made us competitive. But she's always been there for me when it counted. I try to be there for her, too."

"She sure came through with bail."

"I feel bad about that. It's money she's saved for fertility treatments. She's desperate to have a child. Been trying for years."

Zack rubbed a thumb against his chest, softening the twinge there. He'd always wanted a family of his own. "Fern will get her money back as soon as you're cleared."

"You, too. I'm not going to leave either of you in a bind by skipping bail."

"No worries here," he told her, though she'd picked up on his thoughts.

"Really? I'm sure you have better things to do than follow me around."

"Not so much. No job, at the moment. Got burned out."

"Is that an accusation?"

Zack glanced at her, and the white-knuckled grip she had on her purse. "I'm saying, I've got some time on my hands. Time I could use to help you."

"Help me? How?"

"By proving your innocence. You are innocent, aren't you?" A question he should have asked back in the courtroom, before signing over his life. He phrased it in an off-hand way, but he really wanted to hear the answer. Needed her word.

"Of course, I'm innocent."

"Good. So let me help."

A smile tugged at her lips. "Think you've read enough crime novels to figure out this yarn, Sherlock?"

She remembered. He wouldn't have thought she'd bothered to check out the books on his bedside table. They'd been too busy on the bed, itself. Maybe she'd noticed when she'd grabbed her stuff and sneaked out the next morning.

"Okay, I'm not a detective. But I do have an insider's take on the crime scene. I helped put out the fire, I was there during the investigation, and I see the fire chief almost every day. I might be able to come up with something useful."

He could feel her gaze on him as she mulled it over. During the silence, he checked his mirrors. Fern was still with them.

"Look, Heather, I know the police will have their eyes on this case—"

"I've heard Josephine Frost is a top-notch investigator."

"Sure." In fact, she'd solved a couple of high profile mysteries last Christmas. "I just don't know how involved Joey is with *this* case. But I've got a personal interest here." That didn't come out right. He didn't want her thinking he was in love with her, or something stupid like that. "I want the answers, too. The *truth*. As a firefighter and a resident of this town."

And as an employee of the place that burned, leaving him jobless. He didn't mention that part to her, though. No sense adding salt to open cuts.

Heather relaxed the hold on her purse. "Turn here. It's the second house on the left."

Zack pulled up in front of the bungalow. It was an older home with a nice wide porch running across the front. A single pine stood to the side, wrapped so tight with electric lights it looked ready to choke.

She opened her door, then turned back and met his gaze. "Thanks for the lift. And for giving me hope."

Heather jogged up the front walk, avoiding the icy patches, then bound up the porch steps to the front door. Two sets of footsteps followed her.

She should have waited for her champions, but she desperately wanted to see Lottie. And, just as desperately, she had to get away from Zack.

Sitting next to him in the truck, without touching him, had been unbearable. She'd kept a tight hold on her purse to make her hands behave.

But she couldn't help reliving that moment in the courtroom, when she'd hugged him—felt the solid strength of him, and that flutter in her chest, that weakness in her knees only Zack's touch produced.

Then he'd turned into a statue.

Heather couldn't blame him. She'd abused their friendship—slept with him and then ran away.

But she'd had to go. Knew she'd be unable to resist if he'd asked her to stay. And she couldn't risk dragging him down with her.

As she knocked on the front door, she heard Christmas music playing inside—*Frosty the Snowman,* one of Lottie's favorites. Heather knocked again.

She was about to check the snow-covered planter for the extra key, when the door opened and Ruth appeared, dressed as if ready to attend a business meeting.

"Oh, it's you," Ruth said. "I thought I heard something. And Zack Jones…what a pleasant surprise."

He gave Ruth a nod as he stomped the snow from his boots. Thankfully, they knew each other. One less introduction for Heather to perform. A good thing, given her mother-in-law's cavalier greeting. Heather was still busy picking her jaw off the handwoven welcome mat. After a night in jail, she'd expected a hug, at least.

"Ruth…this is my sister, Fern."

"Well, let's not stand here heating the yard." Ruth opened the door wider. Once they were all inside, the older woman went to the hall closet and grabbed a hanger. She held out her free hand to take Heather's coat. "I didn't expect you so soon. Did they drop the charges against you?"

"No, unfortunately. But, with a little help from my friends, I managed to make bail."

Ruth's gaze bounced between Zack and Fern. "That's fantastic." Her smile withered. "Does this mean you're taking Lottie back to Burlington with you? I already called The Hopportunist to let them know you needed some time off and would phone when you were available again."

How thoughtful. Heather wondered how much damage control she'd have to do with her boss. "Well…since they're not expecting me, I may as well hang around town." If she and Zack were going to do some snooping, Carol Falls was the best place to start.

Ruth's smile made it to her eyes. "Wonderful. You and Lottie are more than welcome to stay here. Help yourself to the guest room, dear. You've still got clothes in the closet from your last visit."

Coats hung, Ruth reached for her own. "Sorry I can't stay to see you settled in, but I'm off to visit Chase."

Had she detected bitterness in Ruth's tone? Her trip wouldn't be necessary if Heather hadn't followed through with the charges against Chase. He was sitting in a prison cell because of her.

On more than one occasion, Ruth had asked Heather to accompany her, and to bring Lottie. Fear held her back. Fear and maternal instincts. She'd always protected Lottie. As long as she drew breath, she always would. Prison was no place for a young child. Especially one as fragile as Lottie.

"The girls are in the living room watching a movie," Ruth said, pointing the way. "Please, go ahead and join them."

As soon as Ruth left, Fern closed in and whispered, "Do you really want to stay here and be reminded of Chase? You're totally welcome to come with me to New York. I'm sure we can get permission from the judge for you to leave Vermont. You and Lottie should be around family. Your *real* family. You need to have some fun. Enjoy yourselves."

True. But Heather needed to prove her innocence first. She reached for her sister's hand. "I really appreciate the offer, Fern. And we will visit. I promise. Once my name is cleared."

Heather peeked around the tall artificial tree that acted as a room divider. Lottie and Wenda, still in their PJs, sat cross-legged in front of the TV, transfixed by the action on the screen. A wood fire crackled in the hearth at their side.

Though it was daytime, the tree's lights blinked, casting red, green and blue spots on the hanging ornaments—all small frames, about two inches square. Each frame held a family photo in it. Many of the shots were of Lottie, at various ages. More were of Wenda—school photos, chronicling her evolution from babyhood to the present day.

Most were of Chase.

First, as a grinning boy with several baby teeth missing. Then as a teen, shining with the kind of good looks a few acne pimples couldn't squelch. Finally, as a man—handsome, confident.

When had he transformed into the person she knew? Or had he hidden that anger from the camera, and from his family, the same way he'd concealed it from her when they'd dated.

Heather noticed her own picture was conspicuously absent in Ruth's home. Hardly her mother-in-law's fault. Heather had never given Ruth a photo of herself. She'd always shied away from the camera. Preferred to be the person behind it, rather than in front of it. That way, she didn't have to explain the bruises.

She stepped past the camouflage of the tree. "Hi, Lottie."

Lottie's head whipped around. "Mommy!" She jumped up, ran across the room and leapt into Heather's waiting arms.

Holding her daughter tight and smelling the sweet scent of her hair made the horror of being caged in a prison crumble in Heather's memory. This is what counted. This is what mattered. She'd do whatever it took to stay out of jail and be with her daughter.

When she looked up, she saw three pairs of eyes on her. Wenda's registered shock, Zack's warmth, and Fern's...

Hers were shrouded. Unreadable.

"Have you come to take me home, Mommy?"

"Actually, Grandma's invited us to stay here for a few days. Would you like that?"

Lottie smiled and gave an enthusiastic nod.

"Or you could visit me," Fern said, threading her fingers through Lottie's hair. "You remember me, don't you, Lottie? I'm your Auntie Fern. Wouldn't you like to go to New York and stay with me and Uncle Doug?"

Lottie's smile vanished. She jerked her hand away and looked at Heather warily.

"She's a little shy—" Heather began, trying to soften Lottie's unintentional slight, but her sister cut her off.

"Maybe some other time then," Fern said, her features hard. "I should be getting back to the city. Keep me posted."

Heather promised to do so. She gave her sister a kiss on the cheek and encouraged Lottie to wave good-bye. That's when the little girl noticed Zack.

Lottie went stiff in her arms and hid her face against Heather's shoulder.

Not again.

Her child had met Zack before. Sure, it had been awhile, but Lottie had a good memory. If she acted like this with people she knew, how would she behave around the complete strangers she'd meet at the upcoming rehearsals?

Zack had seen the same reaction from other kids—covering their eyes, figuring if *they* can't see you, *you* can't see them.

No problem. He knew how to get her attention.

He reached into the front pocket of his jeans and found a quarter. He held it in his palm, squeezing his thumb in so that the coin stayed glued to his hand.

By now, Ruth's daughter had wandered over to them. A ready-made volunteer for his demonstration.

"Hi," he said to the black-haired girl. "Your name's Wenda, right?"

"Yeah. Wenda Connolly."

"I'm Zack...one of the firefighters in Carol Falls." Most people trusted smoke jumpers, so he led with his best. "I hope I'm not out of line, but I notice you've got something shiny in your ear..."

He reached behind her head, ensuring the back of his hand faced his audience. Then he let the coin drop to his fingers and drew away, palm forward this time, so it would look like he'd pulled the coin from Wenda's ear.

"That is so neat," the teen said. "Lottie, see what Zack can do."

The little girl peeked at him, but held tight to her mother. Zack couldn't blame Lottie. Snuggling close to Heather was a favorite fantasy of his.

"Do it again, Zack."

He snapped out of his daydream and focused on the teen. "Not sure if there's anything else in your ear, Wenda, but I'll check." He pretended to drop the coin into his other hand, and into his pocket. But, really, he had it palmed, ready to go for a second time.

He performed the same trick, reaching behind Wenda's ear and revealing the silver coin for all to see. Lottie's eyes were about twice the size of the quarter.

"Awesome." Wenda gave him a high-five. "Can you do other tricks?"

"A few." He knew a ton, but didn't want to brag.

"Can you come to our rehearsal this weekend and show the kids?"

Zack had read all about the Winter Recital, and Wenda's participation in it, from the local newspaper. "I could be persuaded," he began. "If you can convince Heather to come out with me and grab a bite."

"Will do," Wenda replied, as Heather shook her head.

"I really need a shower and—"

"I know you want to spend time with your daughter today. I'll be here at nine tomorrow morning to pick you up for breakfast."

He'd meet with Heather over eggs and create a game plan to clear her. If nothing else, a shared investigation would keep her in his sights.

As long as he remembered to look with his eyes, and not with his hands.

CHAPTER FIVE

The next morning, Zack arrived early. The sooner he met with Heather, the sooner they could prove her innocence, and he could collect the bail money he'd put down for her.

It had nothing to do with her smile. Or the way she'd kissed him that night a year ago.

Nothing at all.

He parked his pickup near Ruth's house and nursed a coffee while he listened to the radio. The country station played Christmas tunes now—oldies like *Two-Step Around the Christmas Tree* and *Grandma Got Run Over By a Reindeer,* as well as newer ones by Luke Bryan and Lady Antebellum.

At first, he tapped out a cheerful beat on his steering wheel. After a few minutes, though, the songs didn't sound so merry. Especially the set that started with Randy Travis singing, *Meet Me Under the Mistletoe.* It reminded Zack he was alone this year. No job, no special woman in his life.

Sure, he could count on his mom for company. And to put on a nice Christmas spread. He'd buy the food and roast the turkey, and she'd handle the rest.

One day he'd have a wife and kids to celebrate along with them. He could imagine his mom with grandchildren—telling them stories, spoiling them with affection.

But not this year.

As far as he knew, the fire chief was on his own for Christmas, too. Zack supposed Sylvia Frost, Ian's aunt, would invite her nephew over for a family celebration. Then again, maybe one of the other firefighters had already asked the boss to join them on the big day. Zack made a mental note to check. If Ian had nowhere to go, Zack's mom was always game to feed another person. Or the two of them could hit the local pub together. Apparently, the Hawk & Hound put on an excellent turkey dinner with all the trimmings on Christmas Eve.

He switched off the radio and cut the engine. It was a mild day but, even so, a chill eventually overtook the truck and penetrated his jacket and sweater. Zack checked his watch. It was close enough to nine for him to look merely early, and not overzealous.

He made his way up the porch steps and knocked. Behind the door, he heard a skirmish—heels on the wood floor and muted voices. The lock clicked and the door swung open to reveal Wenda, dressed in leggings and an oversized, tie-dyed T-shirt that read ARTISTS ARE COLORFUL.

"Heather'll be right down. Come on in."

Zack stomped the snow from his boots then entered the foyer. "Nice shirt."

Wenda beamed. "Thanks. My mom made it for me."

They both looked up when Heather appeared at the top of the stairs. "Am I late?"

"No. I'm early." Zack cleared his throat. "Only by a few minutes."

She was beautiful, her smile fragile, like a delicate doll. And her sweater...

"That's a nice color on you," Wenda told her.

Zack concurred. The rosy number suited Heather's creamy skin and made her eyes look bluer. He stared at her for an entirely different reason, though.

"It's pretty mild out," he said, once he found his voice again. "You might be hot in that."

"Oh." She stopped mid-flight and peeled the garment over her head, reminding him of how she'd removed that same sweater a year ago. That time, she'd thrown it on the chair in his bedroom...before taking off a whole lot more.

Zack wiped his forehead.

"It *must* be hot," Wenda agreed. "You're sweating."

Darn teenager didn't miss a thing. Served him right for showing up before nine.

Heather saw it in his eyes. He'd recognized the sweater.

Damn, the man didn't miss a thing.

She'd worn it a year ago, on the night of the staff Christmas party. They'd danced, kissed under the mistletoe, and kissed all the way back to his place.

She hoped he didn't think she'd worn the sweater for old time's sake. She'd craved an extra layer to warm the chill she still felt from that prison cell. Thankfully, she had a turtleneck shirt underneath. Otherwise, shedding the offensive piece would have thrust her into the realm of Dita Von Teese.

Wenda picked up the discarded sweater from the bannister and ran her hand over the wool. "Mohair. Nice."

"Try it on, if you like." Loaning the sweater to Wenda was the perfect way for Heather to send a message to Zack that she didn't value the garment as memorabilia. "Growing up, Fern and I used to swap clothes all the time. And the two of us are sisters, by marriage."

"You sure?"

"Sure." It was an item she'd kept at her mother-in-law's for emergencies. Too nice to toss, too filled with memories of her night with Zack to wear.

She'd thought about giving it away the morning after they'd been together. But when she'd chucked it in a bag for the drop box, she'd caught a whiff of his sandalwood cologne, relived those moments they'd spent together, then hung it back in the closet.

From the way he looked at her now, she knew she'd have to set some rules. He needed to understand nothing was going to happen between them. She valued him as a friend, but their relationship wasn't going to go beyond that. She had other priorities.

"In fact, Wenda, keep the sweater. You're welcome to it."

The teen looked at the thing as if it were crafted from pure gold. "Wow. Thanks."

Heather pulled on her coat and then slipped into her boots. "I won't be long."

"Where are you going, Mommy?" Lottie peered around the Christmas tree, her brows furrowed.

The apprehension in her daughter's voice killed Heather. As a parent she had to reassure Lottie it was okay for them to be apart. It didn't mean she'd disappear forever.

"I'm going out to shop for your Christmas presents. I'll be back later, angel. I promise." She kissed her little girl and joined Zack at the door.

He opened it for her, then opened the car door after that. He'd always treated her like a lady. Something Chase had done, too.

At first.

Zack cranked up the heat and headed toward the shops in the Main Square. "I thought we'd grab breakfast at Kate's and figure out our game plan."

Heather pictured the amount of money she had in her wallet. "As long as we split the bill. Since this isn't a date."

There, she'd said it. She couldn't be clearer than that.

He glanced over at her, a confident smile growing. "Believe me darlin', if I take you on a date, you'll know it."

His voice was low...sexy...and she remembered how her insides had melted at his touch. *Oh, yeah. She'd know it, all right.*

"You perform magic tricks for your dates?" she asked, joking to cool the sexual heat between them. But her joke had the opposite effect on her...because it was true. He'd done amazing things with his hands.

"I liked magic as a kid. Saw a guy on TV pull a coin out of someone's ear. Thought if I could do that for real, I could help my mom with the household expenses."

Thank goodness her question hadn't triggered the same sultry memories for him as it had for her. He'd taken it as an invitation to tell her about himself. How like a guy.

"It was only the two of you?"

"Yeah. My dad died when I was really young. I don't remember him. Well, hardly." He was silent for a moment, as he turned the corner onto the Main Square.

"At one of my first fires, there was this young boy. He was really scared. Wouldn't talk. Just shook. We needed to know if there were other people in the house, but no one could get through to him. Until I remembered that coin trick. I was rusty, but I pulled a quarter out of my pocket and did it for him. He was so intrigued, he forgot to be scared."

Zack's smile faded. "Long story short, he told us his little sister was still in the house and where to find her bedroom. Their parents had gone out to look for after-Christmas sales and figured the two kids would be okay at home, unsupervised."

"That's terrible."

"Some folks don't think. Thankfully, those parents didn't have to pay for their mistake with their children's lives."

"Your magic trick saved the day."

"That and the excellent volunteer firefighting team we have here in Carol Falls." He pulled into a parking spot near Kate's Kitchen. "Since then, I've seen magic work on adults, too. Helps take their mind off the immediate fear. So I've brushed up on all those tricks I used to know, and even added a few more to my repertoire."

When he turned off the ignition, Heather opened the passenger door. Before she had her seatbelt off, he'd whipped around to help her out of the truck. Then he proceeded to open the door to Kate's for her. A girl could get used to this treatment.

Heather loved the interior of the diner, decorated in Kate's own eccentric style. Mismatched furniture and fanciful Christmas decorations filled the foreground, while Kate's travel photos papered the walls, chronicling her earlier life as a journalist.

The smells were even better—cinnamon, bacon, coffee and toast—reminding Heather she hadn't had much to eat since that muffin she'd had the day before. A night in jail had stolen her appetite. But now, with all the delicious aromas, her stomach grumbled. Luckily, she doubted Zack heard it over the festive Christmas music and murmured conversations of the customers. He grabbed a table near the front of the diner, helped her out of her coat and held out a seat for her. A waitress came by, filled their cups with hot coffee, and offered them menus.

Heather recalled when she worked for Kate. Briefly. Strange to be on the receiving end. Heather was usually the one serving tables and pouring drinks.

"See anything appealing?" Zack asked, glancing at her over the menu.

Yes. *Him*. With those smoldering brown eyes and a smile that made her feel she was the only woman in the world.

She focused on the menu. "Maybe some sourdough toast."

He didn't reply. When she looked up, he was staring at her.

"Toast? That's all you want?"

When she'd been with Chase, he'd done the ordering for her. Usually, something that didn't contain too many calories. "Yeah.

That'll be good."

Zack shrugged, then signaled to the waitress, drawing her to their table. "Sourdough toast for the lady. And I'll have the Mountain Man Breakfast—eggs over easy with an extra order of bacon on the side. Make my toast sourdough, too, please."

The waitress nodded, smiled and retrieved their menus. With the table cleared, Zack expanded, his wide shoulders filling out today's rust V-neck pullover and making the table look narrow.

"So let's talk about your case. Did your lawyer give you any leads?"

Heather repeated what Spence told her about the two witnesses, the key, the lost earring and how, with her breaks strung together that night, she'd theoretically had enough time to make the round trip from Burlington to Carol Falls, steal money from Billy's safe, and cover her tracks by setting fire to the bar.

Though, if she'd really done all that, she hadn't covered her tracks at all. The police still arrested her, certain she'd stolen the cash to improve her lifestyle as a single parent.

"You could have lost the earring while working at Billy's last year."

"Maybe." But she was pretty sure it went missing after she left Carol Falls. Only to show up at the bar now. A rather unlikely coincidence. "Could be someone who looks like me committed the crimes."

"Someone who had a key to the bar? That list would include most of the waitresses."

"And Billy only hires tall blondes."

"None half as beautiful as you, though."

The compliment made her uneasy. Yes, it felt as if a burst of sunshine shone through the clouds but, in Heather's life, such clouds usually threatened storms. She sent him a cautioning look.

"'I cannot tell a lie,'" he said, clearly quoting George Washington's admission to his father about that famous cherry tree. Zack's broad grin dissolved. "Hey, maybe the witnesses did."

"Did what?"

"Tell a lie. About you."

"Why would they do that? Spence went on about Mrs. Trivett being such an upstanding citizen."

"Maybe she's protecting the real arsonist."

"Who?"

Zack took a sip from his coffee. "Connor," he said, at last.

Heather didn't know the young man. Still, she couldn't imagine it. "Why would he start the fire?"

"I have no idea. Maybe he's a pyromaniac."

"Did he ever come into the bar?"

"Sure. For an occasional beer. He definitely could have seen your photo hanging on the wall and accused you to shield himself."

"His grandmother identified me, too."

"Connor's her blood. Sometimes people lie to protect a loved one."

Heather understood that. She'd do anything to protect Lottie. But that didn't explain the reappearance of her missing earring.

The server arrived with their food. Zack's plate overflowed with eggs, home fries, and pancakes. He poured a liberal dollop of Frost Maple Syrup on the latter.

While he dug in, Heather smoothed a thin layer of strawberry jam on her toast, and mulled over Connor's possible motives. She leaned closer and whispered. "Do you think he was trying to kill his grandmother to collect an inheritance?"

"He led her out of the building that night, so that won't wash."

"Could he have stolen Billy's money?"

"The safe showed no signs of tampering. Someone who knew the combination opened it."

"Which brings us back to one of the waitresses."

"Doesn't make much sense to me. They'd have the money in the safe—several thousand, probably—but they'd be out of a job after wrecking the place. Better to grab the money and run."

Heather took another bite of toast and chewed over the information. "Have any of them left town?"

"Not that I've heard. And it doesn't explain why two witnesses identified you."

"True." She wiped the breadcrumbs from her fingers with a napkin. "How much do you know about Connor?"

"I never saw him getting cozy with any of the waitresses, so I don't think he teamed up with one of them to commit the crime, if that's what you're thinking."

"Could he have learned the combination by watching one of the employees? Could someone have told him the right numbers to use?"

"I suppose either scenario is a possibility."

Though neither option gave them a realistic lead. Heather wrapped her hands around her mug, seeking comfort.

"Do you remember the combination of Billy's safe?" Zack asked between mouthfuls.

"Let me see." Heather closed her eyes and imagined herself opening it. She reeled off the numbers to him.

"Correct. Too bad." He slanted his head to one side. "Or maybe that's a plus. A guilty person would lie about it."

"I'm pretty good with figures. Comes from being a waitress. You have to remember prices, table numbers, how many people are in each party…"

"Speaking of figures," he began, moving the plate containing his extra bacon to the center of the table. "I think I ordered too much. Help me with some of this, will you?"

The calorie-packed food smelled divine. She lifted a strip of bacon to her mouth, took a bite and nearly swooned at the smoked hickory flavor.

"I can't eat all three eggs, either." He plopped one on her plate.

She devoured it, soaking up the runny yoke with an extra piece of his toast, and a scoop of his home fries. "Do you usually order more than you can eat?"

He sat there smiling at her. It took her a second to realize he'd purposely upsized his breakfast.

"You tricked me."

"I'm taking care of you."

She held back the salty tears stinging her nose. "Thank you."

"My pleasure."

His hand touched hers, rested there—reassuring and solid. For a moment, the room melted away and it was only the two of them, sitting near the window, holding hands.

Vaguely, she noticed the atmosphere around them change. She could make out the lyrics of the current song perfectly. Had someone cranked up the volume?

When she looked around, she realized most of the chatter in the diner had stopped. The waitress who'd served them stood at the center of the restaurant, a newspaper in her hand, comparing Heather to her photo on the front page. Then came the whispers…

"She's the one."
"She did it."
"The gall of her to show up in Carol Falls."
"That's the woman who set fire to Billy's."

Heather's cheeks burned. She turned to Zack, who bolted to his feet, retrieved her coat and held it out for her.

"Time for us to get moving," he said.

Hurrying, she stuffed her arms in her coat sleeves and clutched her purse.

Zack threw money on the table and hiked his jacket over his shoulder. He led her to the door, then stopped and turned back to the gossiping patrons.

"In this country…people are innocent until proven guilty."

Zack kept a tight hold on Heather, every muscle in his body primed for a fight.

He couldn't believe some of the people in this town. Were they always so judgmental? Had he missed that trait until now?

"Sorry, Zack. Could you slow down a bit?"

He came to an abrupt stop and looked at Heather—her face flushed, her lungs working overtime. Only then did he realize he'd practically dragged her down the street in his flurry to get away from the diner.

"Sorry. I was angry."

"I could tell. Thanks for sticking up for me."

A light snow fell around them, flakes landing on her hair. One perched on her nose, and he had an impulse to kiss it away. Zack exhaled and rid himself of that notion.

"I wouldn't be helping you if I didn't believe in your innocence. It's ludicrous that you'd come back a year later, steal from the bar and set fire to it."

"So it's logistical for you? You believe I'm innocent because the timing of the crime doesn't work for you? Not because you believe in me as a person?"

Sounded like he was about to get himself in trouble with a debate he didn't begin to understand, so he said nothing.

"If Billy's had been robbed and torched the night I left Carol Falls a year ago, would you have believed me guilty then?"

The question caught him off-guard. It certainly would have

made more sense for her to commit the crimes last December.

Heather's expression hardened. "That's what I thought." She pulled away and headed in the opposite direction at a jog.

He ran after her, catching up before she reached the next intersection. Zack drew her into an alcove—a space so tight they ended up chest to chest.

"I wouldn't have believed it then, either. Yesterday, you proclaimed your innocence. Gave me your word. Is there a reason I should doubt it?"

"No, but last Christmas—"

"You left town, yes. In a hurry. And I know why."

Because they'd gone too far, too fast.

He scrubbed a hand over his face, reluctant to admit to the fear that had floated around his brain for the past year. She'd left because she didn't want a relationship with him, and didn't know how to let him down gently.

In sync with his thoughts, she reached up a hand and laid it soft against his cheek. He'd put his heart out on his sleeve and she'd seen it. Now, she felt sorry for him.

Great.

Zack turned away. That's when he saw Connor Trivett with his grandmother. Both stood outside the beauty parlor, the college-aged man pressing buttons on his phone. If there were ever a golden opportunity to question the witnesses, this was it.

"Wait here for me."

"What are you going to do?"

He jaywalked across the street and strode over to the youth. "Connor?"

The young man took a step back. "Oh...uh...hi, Zack."

"How's the hip, Mrs. Trivett?"

She looked up, her eyes dull. The poor woman had been through so much. First surgery, then the fire. Between the painkillers and the trauma, she probably wasn't in the best mental shape. Though she was still feisty enough to appear for her regular hair appointment.

"*W-w-w*e're okay," Connor finally managed to say. "We're staying with Mrs. White."

Zack knew the woman. She was an old friend of the Trivett family, who lived close to Billy Boy's. She sometimes babysat the

Belmont kids, despite her rheumatism.

"Good." Zack cut the distance between them. "I had a few questions for you about what happened the night of the fire."

"Best to leave the questioning to us, Zack," a voice behind him said.

Zack turned to see the Deputy Police Chief, Josephine Frost, and her partner, Officer Noel Fletcher. The willowy blonde and the ex-military man, both in uniform, stood with hands on hips.

"Just making conversation," Zack replied, cursing his luck at running into a pair of cops on patrol.

Fletch gave him a tight smile. "As long as that's all. Your presence is a little intimidating, Zack. Wouldn't want to have to arrest you for witness tampering. Or jaywalking." He stepped forward, and lowered his voice. "I see Heather Connolly over there. Did she put you up to this?"

"Of course not." Zack looked across the street. Heather was right where he'd left her—motionless and tense.

"Good. Witness tampering is a serious charge and comes with a hefty fine and jail time.

"Best to let the officers of the court do their job," Joey added. "Leave the amateur detective stuff to Scooby-Doo.

Out of the corner of his eye, Zack caught Connor's relief. The young man scampered into the beauty parlor on his grandmother's heels.

With his witness gone and the watchful eyes of the cops on him, Zack needed to find another way to get the information he wanted.

Scooby-Doo never had it so bad.

CHAPTER SIX

Zack jammed his hands into the pockets of his jacket and marched back to Heather. He opened the passenger door of his truck and helped her in.

"I take it that didn't go well," she said once he'd slipped behind the wheel.

He gave her the short version of his encounter with the officers. "If I noticed Mrs. Trivett's condition, Joey and Fletch must have, too. I bet they'll follow up and review her witness statement. Check for coercion."

"Maybe. But after being falsely arrested, I'm afraid I don't have much faith in the police." She hung her head low. "And, with our investigation over…"

He hated to see her disheartened. Hadn't realized how much their independent sleuthing meant to her morale. "Who said it was over?"

Knowing they couldn't ask questions of the witnesses cut their options. At least downtown and so close to the police station.

"I've got another idea. It involves us, the fire truck and some Christmas lights."

She lifted her gaze to him, her eyes wide. "An interesting mix. Do tell."

Zack eased the truck in to traffic on the Main Square and made his way to the covered bridge that led to the other side of Carol Falls. "Last year, I came up with the idea of decorating the fire truck with lights and driving it around town on Christmas Eve. Everyone got a kick out of it. Especially, the kids."

"I bet. That would be something to see."

Except she'd missed it, because she had left town. "You'll see it this year."

Heather didn't reply. Obviously, she planned to return to Burlington as soon as she could.

No problem. It wasn't like anything was holding her here. Or to him.

"How does decorating the fire truck help us get information?"

"It doesn't. But talking to Ian might."

"Who's he?"

"Our chief, and we're lucky to have him. We've had several bad fires in the past few years. Some deliberately set." Zack replayed a particularly sad case in his mind. "Your lawyer and his fiancée witnessed one of those blazes in the spring."

She went quiet, again. He shouldn't have mentioned Spencer Frost and reminded Heather of her legal woes. When they got to the fire station, he parked on the street and reached for her hand.

"Look, we've had a setback, but I'm going to keep trying. Talking to Ian might give us the clue we're looking for."

They left the truck and made their way to the entrance of the red-bricked fire hall. Zack poked his nose into the chief's office, but Ian wasn't there. Hearing a 'hello' from the second floor, Zack started up the steps.

"Is there a washroom here?" Heather asked.

"Sure." He pointed to the door at the top of the stairs.

"Great. I suspect you'll find out more if I'm not around, anyway."

"I'll meet you back downstairs. Feel free to scope out the fire truck and the other emergency vehicles. They're pretty cool."

He left her behind in the hall and entered the large common area—part kitchen, part meeting room. Long tables formed a rectangle with chairs all around. This is where the volunteers gathered, where Ian held training classes, and where they explained fire safety to kids, hopefully in an entertaining way.

Ian sat at one of the tables, framed by stacks of files. The boss shuffled some paperwork to conceal the document he'd been reviewing, but not before Zack noticed the words 'Divorce Decree'.

Zack kept his mouth shut. Although he'd known Ian for the better part of a year, he knew next to nothing about him personally. Only four things, in fact. That Ian came from New York. That he'd wanted a change of pace. That he'd heard about the chief's job in Carol Falls from his aunt, Sylvia Frost. And that Ian spent a lot of time at the Frosts' maple sugar farm—even boarded there, since the volunteer fire department wasn't built with overnight stays in mind.

If the chief wanted to reveal more, Zack would willingly listen, but he wasn't going to grill the man about his private affairs. Rooting around in the past was a messy, messy business.

"You were right about the cause of the fire at Billy Boy's, Schwartz."

Sweet. Ian was in a talkative mood. "The plastic lamp?"

"With newspapers layered on top of the shade, the set-up provided a makeshift timer. The bulb burned hot and ignited, more or less on cue."

"After the thief stole the money and escaped."

"Exactly."

"If the place had burned to the ground, it might have taken us awhile to locate the safe and discover the theft."

"Maybe that's what our fire-starter planned."

Zack couldn't imagine Heather concocting such a plot. At least, not the Heather he knew.

As he mulled over the information, he heard whistling. The thud of footsteps on the stairs added a bass beat to the airy tune. A second later, Jim Frost stuck his head in the room.

"Hi, Ian…Zack."

Apparently, the Frosts were out in full force today. Zack had already run into Joey and now her older brother, Jim, was making an appearance.

Like his sister, and eldest sibling, Garret, Jim was tall. Both brothers had hazel eyes and dark hair, though Jim sported a longer, rock star length.

And, as Zack recalled, he'd had a run-in with Jim, too. About the same time last year. Zack had been protecting Heather then as well, come to think of it. Though any posturing between Zack and Jim was well over now. In the months since Jim had moved back to Carol Falls, he and Zack had become friendly. Not exactly pals, but certainly not adversaries.

"What have you been up to, ol' man?" Jim asked, addressing his slightly older cousin.

"This morning, I got roped into delivering Christmas baskets with your folks."

Zack knew about the program. Each December, the Frost family donated gift baskets to the poorer residents in Carol Falls. Each basket contained much needed food and most appreciated presents. When Zack was young, he and his mother had once been recipients of the Frosts' generosity.

"That room over the family garage has become Grand Central Station," Jim said, his eyes twinkling. "First, Spencer was there, now Ian has it. The place must have a revolving door."

As they shared a laugh, Zack noticed the green flyer in Jim's hand. "Whatcha got there?"

"I came to invite Ian to the Hawk & Hound on Monday. Now I can invite you, too, Zack."

"You're playing an extra night?" Always musical, Jim had a regular gig at the pub, singing and accompanying himself on the guitar. Zack had seen him perform on the occasional Saturday when he'd dropped by for a helping of shepherd's pie.

"The owner wants to drum up more business on his slow nights, so he asked me to give Monday a try, and I don't want to play to an empty house."

"I'm sure April will be there," Ian assured him. Jim had married his high school sweetheart this past spring and became an instant dad to her adopted son, Marcus.

Zack took the flyer. Maybe Heather would like to go. After all the stress she'd been under, it would be a great way for her to unwind. "Sounds like a solid project."

"Speaking of which—" Ian said "—how goes that *other little* project you've been working on, Jim?"

Zack assumed he meant rebuilding Billy Boy's, until Jim got a dopey look on his face.

"April and I have been trying to add to our family," he explained.

"I'm not surprised you haven't had any success yet," his cousin said. "You're working the maple sugar business, doing private contracting six days a week, and playing at the Hawk & Hound. Your baby-making potion is plain tired."

Jim blushed but chuckled along with them. The man might be tired, but he'd never looked happier—doing exactly what he'd always dreamed of, with a loving wife at his side.

Zack envied him. He wanted that kind of life too, but had never found the right woman.

With one notable exception.

And where was she? Still in the restroom? Zack knew some women took hours in there, but she must have heard Jim's voice, and they definitely knew each other. Why didn't she come out and say hello?

He was about to go find her when Jim slapped his hand on the table, as if struck by an idea.

"Hey, are you free two Saturdays from now?"

The way Zack figured it, he was free as a bird until Billy Boy's was up and running again. "Looks that way."

"My brother needs a bartender for his wedding. Interested?"

"I thought Garret was supposed to marry Lily this past summer."

"That was the first plan, but Lily hadn't spoken to her folks for a while. Garret wanted to rectify that before the wedding, so he and Lily went on a bunch of trips back and forth to Denver to meet with her parents and sister. Everything's good now."

Zack had no idea Lily had been estranged from her family. Jim's expression suggested there was a lot more to the story. Though, again, Zack didn't ask. Not his place.

"Lily thought a Christmas wedding would be perfect, too—since that's also when she and Garret got engaged. They had people all lined up to work it, but a lot have come down with the winter flu that's going around."

"I'd be happy to help out."

"Fantastic. I'll let them know. And, if you don't have anything planned for this week, I could use a hand on a construction site."

Was Jim offering him work to be nice? Did it matter? Zack had enough money saved to tide him over for a while. At least, he did, until he'd helped Heather make bail. At this point, he wasn't in a position to turn down a paying job. In fact, it was about time he started looking for a permanent one.

"Doing what?"

"Updating a couple of bathrooms for the Whites. Their kids want me to replace the old counters with quartz, and to install a walk-in tub for Mr. White, who's having mobility issues. The renos will be this year's Christmas gift for their parents. I could use some extra muscle for the heavy stuff and, Lord knows, you've got muscles to spare."

The little house would be a crowded spot with the renos, the Whites and their two guests—Mrs. Trivett and her grandson. Being there might give Zack another opportunity to ask Connor a few questions. Without the police knowing about it.

"Thanks for thinking of me."

Jim shook Zack's hand, and then looked at the wall clock. "That was the last flyer I had to deliver. Now that I've got the rest of the afternoon free, maybe I'll get to work on that *other little* project we mentioned."

They laughed again. Zack followed Jim to the door, glancing back in time to see Ian's lightheartedness evaporate as he retrieved those divorce papers and stuffed them back into their envelope.

Heather listened to the men's laughter from the safety of the bathroom. She'd been about to emerge when she'd heard Jim's familiar whistle. After what happened the previous Christmas, she couldn't face him again.

She should have explained it all to Zack when she'd had the chance. He'd said he understood why she'd left town, but did he really? Had he and Jim talked about her?

If that were true—if Zack knew what really happened, Heather couldn't imagine he'd be so willing to help. Worse, his good image of her would be destroyed.

That was enough to decide the issue. She'd be better off keeping her past with Jim to herself. At least, for now.

Once she heard Jim leave, she tiptoed downstairs and met up with Zack. He repeated the information he'd learned from Ian, and then gave her a thorough tour of the station—showing her their vehicles, their equipment and their safety gear. Afterward, he retrieved the Christmas lights and, together, they decorated the fire truck.

She wished Lottie were with them. Her little girl would love to see all the colorful lights.

Heather was about to tell Zack she should be getting back, when his hand clasped hers. "You're missing Lottie, aren't you?"

Amazing how well he knew her.

"I'll drive you to Ruth's. I don't think we're going to learn anything more today. Let's sleep on it and come up with a new plan."

As they traveled along in his red pickup, Heather fantasized about a life with her daughter that didn't involve courts and lawyers and fear. She imagined Lottie helping her decorate a tree in a sweet little house of their own. One Zack shared.

But that would never happen.

She'd have to settle for his friendship. Convince herself it would be enough. At least, while she battled the courts.

And as long as she held onto her secret.

CHAPTER SEVEN

Sunday morning brought sunshine. It peeked through the frosty window of Ruth's guest bedroom, giving the walls a soft, buttery glow.

With the house quiet, Heather closed her eyes again and tried to doze. She'd had trouble falling asleep after the excitement of the previous night.

Ruth and Wenda had insisted on taking them to the River of Light Parade in Waterbury. Heather would have preferred to hole up at the house but, once in the middle of the festivities, she was glad of the distraction, marveling with Lottie at the sights and sounds.

People from the community—young and old alike—paraded with lanterns constructed from willow and tissue paper. Heather saw three-foot birds, multicolored fish, buildings, a plane, even a beach-ball-sized Earth—all displayed on poles and lit from inside with battery-operated LED lights. The event culminated with fire jugglers twirling their burning sticks to the drumbeat of a live band, delighting the crowd of onlookers.

Heather had planned to take her daughter to the Santa Claus Parade in Burlington. But, like many youngsters, Lottie feared the big elf in the red suit, and refused to sit on the Mall Santa's knee and have her photo taken. The River of Light Parade was a wonderful alternative.

Beside her in the bed, Lottie stirred, then whimpered. Her head lobbed from side to side and her limbs twitched, as if she were trying to get away from something.

Another nightmare.

Heather wrapped her arms around her daughter. She could feel

Lottie's heart beat like the wings of a trapped bird.

"It's okay. It's okay, honey."

The little girl's eyes sprang open, the whites showing.

"Mommy's right here," Heather whispered, as she rocked her child. "I won't let anything bad happen to you. Ever."

Heather lived by that promise. During her marriage to Chase, she'd protected Lottie from his temper. Whenever he geared up for an explosion, she'd ask Lottie to play in her room, or outside.

She'd save Lottie from the nightmares, too.

Heather hummed one of their favorite tunes—*Let it Go* from the movie *Frozen*. She wasn't much of a singer and hit a lot of bad notes, but Lottie never seemed to mind. It didn't take long for her to join in, filling in any forgotten lyrics with *la-la-la*.

The morning sing-a-long worked its magic. Afterward, they cuddled in bed and listened to the gentle wind blowing outside, the sounds of a household waking…and the bang of the front door as Ruth and Wenda left early to set up for the day's rehearsal.

Once Lottie had her smile back, they crawled out of bed, washed and dressed. Lottie picked a pink, corduroy jumpsuit that Ruth designed especially for her. Heather, on the other hand, had a limited wardrobe at her mother-in-law's house. She hiked up a pair of stand-by jeans with a belt and poked her head into another turtleneck—baby blue, this time.

While her daughter ate cereal, Heather downed a cup of coffee and checked her phone messages. She'd called her boss and left a voicemail letting him know her availability. She could use a full week of waitressing to make up for the days she'd lost—especially this close to Christmas—but he hadn't responded yet.

Bundled in their coats, hats and boots, she and Lottie stepped into the winter wonderland outside. It was too chilly to walk to the school's auditorium, so they rode the local bus to the rehearsal. It took them the long way around town—past the pretty little church with its high steeple, and the park, where several adults were helping young children take their first, tentative steps on the skating rink.

The downtown area looked like a scene from a Hallmark movie—the very picture of Christmas with its sparkling decorations and old-fashioned charm.

Heather sighed. She'd missed the place. More than she realized.

All too soon, the trip was over. In spite of their extended ride, Heather and Lottie still arrived at the school early. Only a few snowy cars dotted the parking lot.

Good. Lottie might feel overwhelmed walking in on a crowd of strangers. Going early would give her time to adjust to the new situation. Unfortunately, it also upped the chances of Heather hearing more town ridicule. She squared her shoulders and readied herself for it.

Entering the school, they discovered a rotund fellow wearing a black suit, a bowler hat and a toothbrush mustache. Lottie pulled away, until the man looked up from his clipboard and spoke.

"Hi, Lottie. Do you recognize me? I'm your Aunt Wenda."

Heather squinted, searching for her sister-in-law beneath the padded costume. "Is that really you?"

"It's me, all right. I'm dressed as Oliver Hardy. Remember, Lottie? I told you about him."

The transformation was remarkable—from young woman to vintage, *male* film star. Wenda even twiddled her tie as Ollie used to in the old black and white movies.

"You're one of the first here." She pointed down the hall. "Go this way to the gymnasium. We're getting everyone to gather there."

Heather and Lottie took Wenda's direction and found the gym easily. They sat on the bleachers and watched as more and more children arrived—parents in tow.

One woman in particular captured Heather's curiosity. She sat observing the arrivals, as well, though she didn't appear to have a child with her. When Heather smiled, the other woman took it as an invitation and made her way over.

"I don't remember seeing you in town before," the redhead said, snagging a seat beside them. "I'm Juliette Armstrong."

"Heather Connolly. And this is my daughter, Charlotte–Lottie, for short. Are you one of the organizers?"

"No, no. Not me." Juliette cocked her head to one side in a whimsical fashion. "I guess I'm more of a spectator. I'm a psychologist, and I'm thinking of using drama in my sessions. Role playing can have positive results in therapy."

Heather remembered seeing a documentary on the subject, but didn't know enough about it to carry on a conversation. "Sounds interesting."

"It really is." Juliette shifted closer. "In Ancient Greece, there was quite a debate about the role of drama in society," she reported, her melodic voice filled with energy. "Many today still hold that what appears on the stage is immoral because it's a lie. The actors are deceiving the audience, pretending to be something they're not."

"Makes sense."

"Until you hear the opposite side of the argument. Since the audience knows they're at a performance, and that the players are *acting*, no one can possibly be misled."

Heather wondered if her own past deceptions were as easy to justify.

A fleeting thought because, at that moment, Zack Jones strode into the room. He wore his winter jacket open, exposing a brown sweater that matched his eyes and hugged his torso. Heather's heart betrayed her by beating a little faster.

Several boys called out Zack's name and ran to him. He'd once mentioned he taught fire safety to kids. No doubt they knew him from that. And what little boy didn't want to be a firefighter?

In these days of equal opportunity, maybe little girls did, too. Heather had seen an article in the Carol Falls newspaper, commenting on how Mrs. Hoadley, a well-loved nineth-grade teacher, enjoyed encouraging her female students to follow their hearts and pursue careers outside the typical gender roles.

Heather doubted waitressing would make the grade.

She shook off those thoughts as she watched Zack greet the children, his smile like a warm embrace. Heather wished he'd turn his gaze on her, so she could feel it, too. Instead, he produced a deck of cards, and it wasn't long before a chorus of "Oooohs" and "Ahhhhs" rose from his audience—now comprised of both boys and several curious girls. Lottie stood, craning her neck to see around them so she could catch Zack's next trick.

"You can go closer if you want," Heather coaxed. "It's okay."

Lottie sat again, concern wrinkling her young brow, as shyness got the best of her.

Heather sympathized with her daughter. She experienced that same nervousness when Sylvia Frost entered the gym. Several women followed the Frost matriarch, including Mrs. Hoadley, Lily

Parker and April Rochester.

Now, April *Frost*.

Heat climbed up Heather's neck and settled into her cheeks. She hadn't expected to see more Frosts here. Especially, the caramel-haired beauty who'd married Jim.

After what happened last Christmas, she'd hoped to avoid April and Jim Frost indefinitely, but Heather couldn't escape the room without drawing attention. She could only sit there and try to fade into the crowd.

"Good morning, everyone," Sylvia began, and went on to introduce herself as the director of the show. "When I was your age," she said, addressing the children, "I loved going to see *The Nutcracker* ballet with my parents. More than anything, I wanted to dance in the show…until I tried on the pointe shoes. That was the end of my ballet career."

Heather chuckled along with the other adults. She'd always felt a bit intimidated by Sylvia. The woman was so elegant, so self-assured. But that joke about the pointe shoes really broke the ice. Or, in this case, thawed the *Frost*.

Sylvia waited for the laughter to subside. "I went back to my sneakers, but I kept right on enjoying *The Nutcracker* performances. So imagine my thrill when Mark Lauder told me he'd adapted the original E. T. A. Hoffmann story into a play, and asked me to direct it."

Heather knew of Mark from the bookstore, a business he owned with his father. The younger man ran marathons and hung out with the equally fit Peter Boychuk, the accountant at Frost Farms. Heather had no idea Mark was a budding playwright.

Sylvia raised her gaze to the rest of her audience. "I wouldn't have considered tackling such a big project without the help of all our volunteers. And, I'd like to give a special thank you to Mrs. Hoadley…my daughter-in-law, April Rochester-Frost…and my soon-to-be daughter-in-law, Lily Parker."

She indicated the blond Public Relations Manager of Frost Farms, who must have agreed to marry Garret during the year Heather was away. "Lily is in charge of publicity and ticket sales, so your parents will need to speak to her about booking their complimentary passes."

What a relief. At least, Heather wouldn't have to talk to April about attending the show.

"And I'm pleased to announce a real treat," Sylvia continued. "Zack Jones is here to show us some of his magic tricks."

Taking that as his cue, Zack borrowed a long, Harry Potter scarf from one of the kids. He looped it over his own head and appeared to tie it in back. Then, with one swift yank on the ends, he held it stretched out in front of his chest, giving the impression it had magically traveled through his body. The kids cheered, as Zack bowed and returned the scarf to its rightful owner.

Mrs. Frost applauded. "Wonderful. Zack will be going from group to group this morning, to show you more magic. But, right now, to get you warmed up for the rehearsal, we're going to break into smaller groups and play some drama games. When I call your name, please go and stand beside April. You'll be in her group."

Sylvia consulted her clipboard. A couple of Belmont kids were first on her list. Heather knew of the family, but she didn't recognize either of the children.

"Nathan Boychuk."

This kid's cheery dimples brought a smile to Heather's lips, even as she cringed inside. Nathan was Billy's nephew.

"Charlotte Connolly."

Lottie ran over to the group, leaving Heather with her mouth hinged open. She'd anticipated a battle to coax her child to join the others. Heather sat back, pleased with the small breakthrough.

"Duncan. Duncan Frost."

Garret's son, his light brown hair sticking out in different directions, stood and hiked up his pants over his skinny hips. He bumped fists with Nathan, both boys crying out an emphatic, "Yes!" Heather surmised they were best buds.

More kids followed, with names Heather didn't know. Then, another familiar one.

"Marcus Rochester-Frost."

A taller boy, who carried a computer tablet, approached warily, though he received a warm greeting from Duncan and Nathan. Marcus tapped the screen a few times, and showed it to the other two boys, who nodded and bumped fists again. Though he was older than the rest of the kids in his company, Heather remembered Marcus was autistic. It made sense that he'd be with April. She was both his adoptive mother and a special needs teacher.

April acknowledged her group with a cheery, "Follow me." She turned and headed toward the big gym doors, Lottie tailing her.

Heather rose, ready to follow, as Sylvia Frost continued to call out children's names—this time, for Mrs. Hoadley's group.

"Worried about your daughter?" Juliette asked.

"She's a little shy. Usually."

"So go with her. No one will mind."

Heather looked around and saw a few parents lagging behind their children, but most had left, happy to leave their kids in trusted hands for the day.

Juliette picked up her purse and notepad. "In fact, I'll come with you. I want to see how the autistic boy handles new stimuli."

They followed the group down the hall and entered one of the classes. All the desks were piled on the windowed side of the room, which cleared a large, free area for the kids, who immediately took to running around in the empty space. Lottie, included.

Duncan slowed to a jog then stopped in front of Heather's daughter. "I know you. From pre-school. What's your name again?"

Lottie answered as the other two boys joined them.

"I'm Duncan," he told her. "And this is my cousin, Marcus. He doesn't talk. He types everything he wants to say." Duncan turned to his other friend. "This is Nathan. He thinks girls are yucky. Ignore him."

He gave Nathan a good-natured elbow to the ribs and both boys giggled.

"You know what?" Duncan continued, still addressing Lottie. "I'm getting a new mommy. Her name's Lily and she's pretty, like you."

Heather smiled. Compliments could only improve her child's self-esteem, and that Duncan was one smooth operator.

April clapped her hands to get everyone's attention. "I can see you've all got energy to burn, so let's start out with a special game of tag. It's the same as regular tag, until I say, 'Slow motion.' Then, everything you do has to be in *sloooow moootion*." April illustrated physically, as she drew out the last two words.

"Everybody ready?" She tapped Nathan on the head. "You're it."

The children let out excited screams and scattered. As Nathan tried to tag someone, he purposely avoided the girls. Heather snickered. In ten years or so, the guy would be actively pursuing them for a date.

When April called out, "*Slow Motion,*" the kids reduced their speed, running as if underwater. Duncan, clearly the cut-up in the group, tripped on the hem of his pants and did a slow-motion pratfall, which broke up the parents as well as the kids.

After they had been running for ten minutes, Heather sensed the children were ready for a change. So did April. She directed them to join hands and form a circle. Once they were in the right formation, she asked them to sit cross-legged on the floor.

"Together, we're going to create a story...each person adding a single word."

Beside Heather, Juliette turned a page in her notepad and continued scribbling.

"All our stories are going to start with, 'Once upon a time,'" April explained. "So, if I start, my word is..." She indicated herself and said, "Once."

She then pointed to Nathan, who sat on her right. "Nathan would say, 'Upon.'"

Marcus, to the right of Nathan, struck a single key on his tablet and turned it around to show everyone a big letter "A".

"Good job, Marcus."

Duncan was next and sang out the word, 'Time', without prompting.

"Well done, Duncan. And around the circle it goes, each person adding one word to create our story. You have to pay attention to everyone's word for it to all make sense. Try not to plan ahead. Just listen and say the first word that pops into your mind. We'll keep going around the circle until we sense the story is finished. Ready to play?"

The kids nodded, eager for their turn.

April began again. Pointing to herself she said, "Once." Nathan added, "Upon." Marcus held up his "A", and Duncan said, "Time."

Quickly grasping the rules of the game, the rest of the children in the circle contributed the words, "There...lived...a." April praised each contribution.

It was coming up to Lottie's turn fast. Heather crossed her

fingers, hoping her daughter wouldn't freeze up.

A little boy formed his hands into claws, and growled. "Scary."

A dark-haired girl thought for a few seconds, then said, "Ogre."

One of the Belmont kids added, "Named."

And then it was Lottie's turn. Without hesitation, she said her word.

"Daddy."

April raised an eyebrow, but none of the kids registered anything odd. They carried on with the story—the word "Daddy" morphing into "Baddy," the next child to use it obviously having misheard Lottie.

But Heather hadn't misheard.

She couldn't swallow, couldn't breathe. Memories flashed before her of all those times Lottie reverted inward. Like today, when they'd seen Wenda in costume. Or when they were at Ruth's house with Fern and Zack. Lottie had resembled a much younger child, shying away from unfamiliar people. Hell, the little girl had hung onto Heather for dear life.

And yet, here she was, happily joining in the games with kids she didn't know...and a teacher she'd never met before.

It wasn't new situations and new faces that scared Lottie. She was fine around Fern. Fine around April, Juliette and the other children, but recoiled from Zack, her Uncle Doug—even Santa.

Because she feared men. Feared them because of her daddy.

Heather made her way to the door and escaped into the hall. She hunched over, hands on thighs and gasped, fighting the heaviness in her chest to squeeze air into her lungs.

"What happened?" a familiar voice asked. Zack touched her arm.

"I didn't protect Lottie. Not like I should have." The recriminations poured from her in jumbled chaos. "I fooled myself. I thought she didn't know. That I was hiding it from her."

The door opened again, and Juliette appeared. "Are you okay?"

Heather chewed her bottom lip, to keep from running off at the mouth again. She wasn't about to spill her guts to a stranger. "A little faint. I'm fine, now. Thanks."

The other woman nodded, her expression grave. "If you ever need to talk to someone..." She produced a business card and handed it to Heather.

Seriously? Heather couldn't imagine sharing her pain with a psychologist. Or finding the money to hire one. She stuffed the card in her purse, along with a used tissue.

"I should get back in there," she said to avoid the worried faces they both wore.

"Lottie's fine," Juliette told her. "See?"

Heather peered through the class window. Lottie held Duncan's hand as the kids paired up to start a new game.

She caught her little girl's eye. Lottie smiled, blew Heather a kiss good-bye and returned her attention to Duncan.

"Why don't you rest? Come back at the end of the day. After all you've been through—"

Heather shot the psychologist a look. "How do you know what I've been through?"

Juliette shrugged. "I saw you on the news."

Everyone knew. Everyone in town. Probably, in the state. Heather wished she could crawl under one of the school desks and hide.

"I'll drive you to Ruth's," Zack offered, giving her a far better exit strategy.

He wrapped a big arm around her waist and led her out of the building. How reassuring to lean on someone, if only for a little while.

She shouldn't get used to it, though. She'd tried using Zack before—to get over Chase. And that had only ended in regret.

CHAPTER EIGHT

Zack cranked up the heat in his truck and stole a glance at the woman in the passenger seat.

She was calmer now. Her eyes had lost that wild, panicked look. But the tracks of her tears were still visible on her pale cheeks.

A few aftershocks from a night in jail were expected, but he'd never seen her like this. Had never seen anyone so...shattered.

He wasn't a complete stranger to the human condition. Wherever booze flowed, emotions ran high. As a bouncer, it was Zack's job to cut people off before it got that far. Step in, defuse the situation, avoid fights, and break 'em up when they erupted.

Anger he understood. Drunkenness and stupidity? He could work with those, too.

Tears? Now, those were scary.

"How're you feeling?"

"Ashamed. Sorry about losing it back there."

Good. She was holding it together. Zack breathed easier and relaxed his grip on the wheel.

"You're entitled," he said. You've gone through a lot in the past few days." In the past few *years*, he suspected.

They'd never really discussed personal issues before. During their friendship, they'd mostly kept it light. He didn't ask, and she didn't volunteer.

Zack flicked off the radio. "What did you mean, when you said you'd kept it from Lottie?"

Heather gazed out the side window. With her index finger, she drew a line down the fine layer of condensation on the glass. The opening created a peephole to the outside world—an arrow slit on a castle wall.

"I thought I had," she said. "Thought I was protecting her. But I wasn't. She knew what was happening, and she's damaged now because of it. I should have left Chase the first time he hit me."

Zack stiffened, as if he'd taken the punch. In spite of the history with his own father, he couldn't understand why any man would strike a woman. Or why any woman would stick around for the abuse.

"Why did you stay?"

"Because...I felt sorry for him."

She felt sorry for *him?* After he hit her? "I don't understand."

"Chase was so shaken, so apologetic. I ended up comforting him, holding him while he cried in my arms."

Heather wiped away more of the condensation, made the gap another finger-width wider. "He promised he'd never hurt me again. I wanted to believe him. And divorce? We'd been married only a few months. I didn't want to admit defeat. I thought if I loved him enough, it would heal him. Make him whole."

Love. Zack knew something about it. The pain it could cause, for one thing. But Heather told her story in an unemotional, detached way, as if she were a reporter, talking about someone else.

Thank God. He couldn't take a repeat of what happened at the school. Every tear was like a knife—cutting him up inside.

"You had no hint about his temper when you met?"

"We met at my parents' church in Montpelier—so, no." A sad smile flickered on her lips. "My mom and dad ran a pretty tight household. Rigid, really. Chase never planned anything. Always lived in the moment. It was so refreshing, so freeing. Until I started to feel like his babysitter. Still, I thought we could make our marriage work."

"So you stuck with it. Honored your vows." Even though Chase didn't. No man ever honored his wife by striking her.

"I thought—hoped—the violence was a one-time deal. An aberration." Heather used the side of her hand on the window to clear a larger opening in the mist. "The second time he hit me was the same—the sobbing, the promises. Again, I believed him— believed his excuses. He was under a lot of pressure at work, he said. Told me his business investments had soured and that he needed me to help financially. I was already working as a bookkeeper, so I took an extra job waitressing part-time."

"You were a bookkeeper? News to me."

"That was before we met. Once my tip money outweighed my regular bookkeeping salary, Chase encouraged me to wait tables full-time."

"That was okay with you?"

"I thought the extra money would help us. Help repair our relationship. But waitressing isn't great for the ego. Most customers are fine, but some don't look at you as a person. They don't even make eye contact."

Strangers regularly avoided Zack's gaze, but because they were intimidated by his size. Not a bad thing for a bouncer. He grasped the gist of her complaint, however. He'd overheard the waitresses talk about it a few times.

"Other customers are downright abusive," Heather continued. "It's as if they take all their aggressions out on you because they can. In the service industry you're...well...a servant. They'd degrade me during the day, and Chase followed up at night."

Heather's coat swished against the truck's upholstery as she turned in her seat to face him. "Billy was always good to me, though. That's why it's so absurd that I'm accused of burning his place. I would never pay him back that way. And the other waitresses?"

She laughed—a harsh, humorless sound. "They were jealous of all the flowers Chase bought me. He'd have them delivered to the bar and the girls would go on about how I had the best husband. Meanwhile, I was dying inside, knowing the truth. That the flowers were a big show."

Zack remembered those bouquets—roses, orchids, tulips in the spring. "Billy used to joke that you could open a florists' shop on the side."

"Not for long. After I had Lottie, Chase stopped bothering with gifts. There were no more flowers, no more apologies, no more promises. By then, he'd convinced me that I brought on the beatings myself. Said I deserved them. That I didn't do things right. That I didn't cook the meals he liked. That I spent too much time and money on Lottie."

"Must have been hell."

"It got worse…when I discovered his big secret."

An affair? An addiction? "What?"

"He'd been out of work for months. Fired for fighting with a co-worker."

"How'd he hide that?"

"He'd made it clear I was never to call him during business hours, so I didn't know. To be truthful, maybe I didn't want to know. Maybe I overlooked the obvious because reality was too painful. He'd leave in the morning, as if he were going to the office, but he'd bum around Montpelier instead. Since he controlled the finances, I never suspected. Didn't realize he'd drained the bank accounts and maxed out all the credit cards until it was too late."

Zack knew about the money. It was one of the few things she'd shared with him before she'd left Carol Falls. He'd had no idea how bad it was, though. He was sympathetic about it—then and now. But, hearing the full story today made Zack's fist bunch up, ready to pound the guy. Would that make him an avenger, or put him on the same level as the man he despised?

He couldn't help but feel a touch of bitterness, too. Zack would have willingly offered Heather his heart. He would have been good to her—gentle and kind. But she'd left him after one night and stayed with an abusive man for years.

"Things didn't get any better after that, I take it."

"No."

He didn't expect her to say more. Figured she was done sharing. Then she took a big breath, one that hitched a couple of times, as though it hurt. Zack forced his shoulders down from around his ears.

"I could tell when Chase was getting close to a blow-up," she said, her words hushed. "The tension was unbearable. It kept building…building."

Between the car's heater and Heather's de-fogging efforts, the window at her side was clear. She gazed out again. "Sometimes, to ease the pressure, I'd do something I knew would send Chase over the edge—serve him peas instead of corn, or leave a dirty cup on the counter. He blamed me for the beatings anyway, so why not? At least that way I could get it over with before Lottie came home from school. But it didn't help. Lottie knew. *She knew.*"

"You did the best you could in a bad situation." He'd heard the tired line in about a hundred low-budget cop movies. Unfortunately, Zack couldn't think of anything better to say.

"Hardly. I felt responsible. So I covered it up. Lying became second-nature to me. And, at first, it was easy. Chase was clever about where he hit me. He'd pick areas hidden by clothes—my stomach, my ribs, my thighs." She slipped her hand back in its glove. "Toward the end, though, he didn't care. He'd punch me in the face."

Zack winced. "Dear God, Heather."

"If I couldn't cover the bruises with makeup, I'd lie and say I tripped over my feet, or that I'd walked into a door. But I couldn't do anything about Chase's words. They were far worse than his fists. More hurtful. He'd tell me I was stupid, ugly and worthless. I started to believe it. I guess I still do. But when he threatened Lottie…"

Zack almost missed a stop sign. He jumped on the brake. "Chase said he'd hurt her?"

"Said she needed to learn who was boss. I'd never been truly afraid of him until then. That beating put me in the hospital. The attending officers asked me to press charges, and I did. To protect Lottie."

Heather's chin sank to her chest. "I should have protected her all along—divorced Chase while Lottie was a baby and petitioned for sole custody."

Zack reached over and held her hand until he needed his to park. When he turned off the ignition they continued to sit there, holding hands.

"Thanks for listening, Zack. I think I just need to get it out in the open. To talk about it with someone."

"Maybe you should see Juliette. She could help you deal with this."

Because, God knew, he sure couldn't. Not if Heather broke down again. By the time he got out of the truck and went around to her side, she was already out of the vehicle.

"I appreciate the ride."

"I'll walk you to the door."

"That's not necessary."

Was she dismissing him now? Had he said something wrong?

Or was she just embarrassed about her confession?

"I want to," he said, then followed her up the front steps and waited while she fished out a key. "You sure you're going to be okay on your own."

"After a hot bath and a nap, I'll be good."

Her hand trembled as she reached up to insert the key in the lock. He took it from her and opened the door himself.

"It wasn't easy for me to tell you those things today. I always worry people are going to..."

When she hesitated, he cupped her chin and raised her gaze to his. "Go on," he said, hoping he was ready to hear the rest.

"I worry people will judge me."

Judge her? All he wanted to do was *hold* her. *Defend* her. "I'll stop by tomorrow. Take you out for dinner."

"You want to be seen with me? After the reaction I got at the diner?"

"That was a few ignorant people. Don't pay any attention to them."

"Still...I'm not ready to have dinner with a man, Zack."

Not after the suffering she'd endured from her ex-husband.

"It won't be anything fancy—just two pals getting together for burgers," he said, hiding his disappointment and downplaying the date-aspect of his offer. "Besides, we need to plan our next move in the investigation. Remember?"

Zack stepped closer, put one hand on her shoulder. Damn, she looked so vulnerable. "If you need me in the meantime, call me on my cell."

"Thanks."

He kissed her forehead. A friendly peck. One you might plant on your mom to wish her happy birthday. At least, that's what he'd intended. With Heather standing so close, and the warmth of her skin on his lips, and her scent filling his lungs, he wanted more.

He slid both arms around her and dipped his head, before his brain clicked in and he realized what a stupid move it would be.

They were buddies. End of story. And she was too messed up right now for him to confuse the situation. She'd responded to his hug. Might even kiss him back. Maybe fall into bed with him, as she had that night a year ago—seeking pleasure from a man's touch, instead of the usual torture.

But it was wrong. She wasn't ready. Mentally, he kicked himself for even thinking about it. For needing it so bad.

Zack retreated and watched her disappear inside, heard the bolt click into place and lock.

He stood there for a moment, while his heartbeat slowed to normal, wishing he knew what to do—what to *say*—to help her.

Zack drove around aimlessly, checking out snowmen on lawns and plastic reindeer on roofs.

Normally, he would have picked up flowers for Heather to cheer her. His friends, Audrey and Finn, would be busy creating Christmas arrangements in their shop, The Painted Tulip. Probably working on the centerpieces for Garret and Lily's wedding, too. Though Zack was sure they'd gladly make time to whip up a bouquet for him.

But after Heather's story, he nixed the idea. He'd never be able to buy a woman flowers again without thinking of Chase's hollow gesture.

On automatic pilot, Zack found himself downtown, close to Romancing the Stone, the jewelry shop where his mother worked. The place had three large display windows—gems glittering out of gold and silver settings. Christmas balls and tinsel wove around the jewelry, with a few wrapped boxes positioned strategically throughout. His mother's doing, Zack guessed. She had a flare for decorating.

He walked in and spotted a customer examining some items, his back to Zack. Edward Northrup, the shop's owner, was standing on the other side of the display case and speaking to the male client in hushed tones.

Zack found his mother behind the cash register, standing on a stepladder and draping a plastic holly bow on some upper shelves. The hem of her standard wool shirt-dress—navy, today—floated up toward her knees.

"Here, Mom. Let me help you with that."

She blew a stray brown curl from her eyes. "No need. I'm almost done." She looped the end of the bow behind the WE REPAIR WATCHES sign, and took Zack's outstretched hand.

"You've got to stop working so hard, Mom," he said, helping her to the floor.

"Sweetie, I'm up and down this ladder all day."

"I meant your driveway. I went to your place early this morning to shovel for you and it was already done."

She folded the ladder and put it away. "Ed shoveled it for me."

"Ed?" Is that what she called Mr. Northrup these days? "Well, I'll still swing over Thursday morning to take your car in for its oil change."

"No need."

Zack wagged a finger at her. "Mom, you've got to keep up with regular maintenance."

"I know that, son, but Ed's offered to go with me. While we're waiting for the car, he's taking me to lunch."

"Be careful, Mom. He's your employer and that kinda sounds like…well…a date."

She patted Zack's cheek and gave him a patient smile. "It *is* a date, sweetie."

He frowned, unsure of how to take the news. His mom never went out with men—even though she'd been a widow for nigh on thirty years.

"How well do you know this guy?" He regretted the question as soon as it hit the air.

His mom put her hands on her hips. "He's been my boss for two years now, Zack. I practically ran the store for him during his late wife's last illness. I reckon I know him extremely well by now, wouldn't you say?"

He had no idea his mom could be so sarcastic. She sassed him like a rebellious teen.

"And don't worry about bringing dinner over on Sunday. I'm fixin' a roast for Eddie, and I'm hoping you'll join us. I want the two of you to get to know each other."

"Sounds serious."

"It's going in that direction, and I couldn't be happier."

Zack glanced at Edward Northrup, assessing him in light of this new information and, in so doing, recognized the male customer—Officer Noel Fletcher.

"He's already purchased a bracelet," his mom said, in a low voice, her Texan drawl softened from all her years in Carol Falls. "Then, on the way out, the engagement rings caught his eye."

According to local gossip, Fletch had reconnected with

Josephine Frost last Christmas. The timing for an engagement was about right. If things had gone as planned for Zack last December, he might well have been in the market for a diamond now, himself.

"Maybe, one day soon you'll be looking for rings, too," his mother said, echoing his thoughts.

"Haven't found my number one lady, yet."

"Well, y'all won't find her attending art movie nights with Audrey and Kate while their brothers are in tow."

Not entirely true. He'd met Robin Redmond at one of those evenings and flirted with her. However, at that time, the pretty, amber-eyed woman was pining over Spencer Frost, while Zack was still trying to douse his torch for Heather. So the innocent flirtation went nowhere.

"How about that girl you used to be stuck on?" his mom asked, again reading him perfectly. "I hear she's back in town."

"And in a whole lot of trouble."

She leaned closer. "Do you think she really set the fire?" Zack could tell by his mother's kind, brown eyes that she didn't. "And her a single mom. She must be worried sick. I know I would have been."

Zack thought about his own youth, and how hard his mom had worked to do it all—support them, and still give him a great childhood. Once, he'd moped around, wishing he had a dad to throw ball with him. A few weeks later, she took him in the backyard of the house they rented and pitched balls to Zack. No girly underhanded stuff for her. No way. She'd worked as a secretary for a trucking company then, and she'd gotten some of the guys to teach her how to throw.

He'd asked her to bake an apple pie one time—now *that* had ended up tasting like sawdust—but she'd tried. As far as moms went, he'd totally lucked out.

"Why don't you get Heather a little something to cheer her up? Maybe some earrings."

He thought about those hooped ones she used to wear. The missing one Connor found.

"We're friends, Mom," Zack said, suspicion nagging him. If Heather was innocent, how did that earring end up at the scene of the crime after all this time?

And, he'd helped her with bail money. How much giving could

he do without looking like a total chump? He didn't want to be the kind of guy who chased after an indifferent woman.

Or an insincere one.

"Something small then. Noncommittal." His mom hummed as she thought. "I know."

He followed her over to a new display. She grabbed a chain, from which dangled a small, egg-shaped mesh. His mom separated the silver spirals, and popped a polished stone inside.

"The pendant is designed so you can put any stone in the middle."

"Neat. But a necklace might seem…"

"Too much? How about a keychain then?" Beside the necklaces, the same silver cage hung from a narrow strip of black leather. "They're not expensive. Under ten dollars. With your family discount, it'd be almost the same price as a latte. Extremely noncommittal. We've already sold a bunch of them for Christmas. Very popular."

The woman could peddle maple leaves to a resident Vermonter. Still, he wasn't a hundred percent convinced. "What kind of stone would I get to go with it?"

She picked up a shiny, white one. "A moonstone would be ideal. It's supposed to bring good luck."

That's exactly what Heather needed. "Okay. I'll take it."

His mom reached behind the counter to grab a box, but Zack stopped her. He didn't want Heather to get the wrong impression. To think he was making some kind of romantic overture.

"Fine, Don Juan," his mom quipped, passing the keychain to him. "The moonstone also brings success in love, so there may be hope for you yet, son."

"Only if I carry it myself," he joked.

Keychain in hand, he thought of another, even better present he could give Heather. One that involved his mother's coffee club—all members of the Ladies' Auxiliary. They'd be at Kate's Kitchen, sharing a cup of java, right about now.

And he always enjoyed one of Kate's Christmas mochas. His good deed bonus.

CHAPTER NINE

Heather spent the rest of Sunday recuperating. Seeing Lottie, excited and happy after rehearsal, lifted her spirts as nothing else could. Yet, that night, the girl's terrors returned with a vengeance—every whimper, every shriek plunging Heather deeper into despair.

Monday, following breakfast, Ruth invited them to go shopping. Though bleary-eyed, Heather hoped a jaunt in the December sunshine would lighten her daughter's evening dreams.

They started at the Cross Roads Market for groceries—where Heather insisted on paying—and ended up at Book Marks. There, a purple-haired clerk helped Ruth select a couple of books for Wenda—both volumes filled with photos of old movie stars.

Heather kept her head down throughout the shopping spree, to avoid drawing attention to herself. No sense setting idle tongues wagging.

When they got back to the house, Heather phoned her boss to get her schedule. He wasn't in, so she left another message, then emailed him again, as well. After all the excitement of the past few days, and several rough nights, Lottie fell asleep watching late-afternoon cartoons.

Heather picked up her sleeping bundle and carried her to the queen-size bed they shared. When she returned to the hallway, she saw Zack at the front door, talking to Ruth.

"Look who's here to take you to dinner," the older woman sang out.

Heather appraised her male caller. With his dark hair mussed, and his brown eyes sparkling, the man stole her breath. Hands down, Zack had more mouth-watering appeal than any of the celebrities in Wenda's picture books.

But, despite his caring and protective nature, despite his skill and passion as a lover, he wasn't emotionally ready for her.

She knew how uncomfortable she'd made him in the car yesterday with her tears, her confession. The man was great at problem solving, cool in a crisis—her lighthouse in the middle of a perfect storm. But when it came to tears, her big, brave warrior crumbled.

And, lately, her world involved one teary crisis after another.

It was different when they'd first met. She'd kept it all buried inside then, suffering in silence. Heather couldn't do that anymore. Couldn't go back to that quiet Hell. And poor Zack didn't need her particular kind of drama in his life.

"Lottie will be hungry when she wakes up," Heather announced. "I should stick around to—"

Ruth swatted the air, and the idea, away with her hand. "I'll make sure the girl is fed. Go on," she coaxed. "Enjoy yourself."

One excuse shot down, and Heather couldn't think of another. As Heather slipped on her coat, Ruth clutched her arm.

"Stay out as late as you want."

What was that supposed to mean? Was her ex-mother-in-law encouraging her to hook up with another man?

Heat rose in Heather's cheeks. This was hardly a date. Surely Ruth knew that by looking at her—outfitted in her old jeans and the same cream turtleneck she'd worn on Saturday. All freshly laundered, at least.

"We won't be long," Zack promised, zipping his jacket over a cobalt blue shirt and his standard black tie. "I gotta run up to Stowe to see my girlfriend after her shift."

Zack had a girlfriend? He'd never mentioned it. But that was good, right? He deserved love in his life.

Then why did Heather feel so disappointed? Even the touch of his hand on her back as he guided her out of the house didn't warm her.

"Is Ruth usually so encouraging?" he asked, once they were in his truck.

"She enjoys her one-on-one time with Lottie."

Heather didn't know what thoughts were pinging around Zack's head, but only one topic of conversation was on her mind.

A topic that was none of her business.

"How long is the drive to Stowe?" A duplicitous question, since she already knew the answer.

"About fifteen minutes."

She waited, expecting more, anticipating some information about this new woman in his life.

"Depending on the traffic and driving conditions."

Drat. That wasn't the embellishment she'd sought. Though, again, where he went and who he saw wasn't her concern.

Apart from the concern of a *friend*, of course. As a friend, she could show interest. Friends talked to one another about their day—what they did, who they saw. Heather wasn't snooping. Honestly. She was encouraging Zack, helping him share.

"What's her name?"

"Who?"

"This person you're seeing in Stowe. Do I know her?"

"No."

Darn. Conversation with this guy didn't used to be this hard. "How do you know?"

"What?"

"How do you know I don't know her?" Now, she was getting tongue-tied. Did that last question even make sense?

"Neither of us know her."

"Excuse me?"

"Neither of us know her, because I made her up. I don't have a girlfriend in Stowe. I said that to get you off the hook...so Ruth wouldn't bug you about me."

He gave her one of those grins that made her knees weak. Good thing she was sitting. It wasn't until she leaned back that she realized how uptight she'd been, how irrational. She kept pushing him away, but didn't want him to be with anyone else. And that smile he'd given her telegraphed that he knew exactly how she felt.

"I'm sorry, Zack. I have no right to pry."

"It's nice to know you care."

"Of course, I care. We..." She almost said *slept together*. Neither of them needed reminding of that. Not with the current flowing between them. "We've known each other a long time, and I appreciate everything you've done for me. But my life is a mess. I already have one failed marriage, I'm facing criminal charges and, as a single parent, my priority is my child. I don't want you to get hurt."

He shifted the car into park and turned off the engine. "Let me worry about that. I'm a big boy."

No argument there. With his wide shoulders and muscular build, he could give Thor a run for his money. Yup, Zack Jones could take on the world. For now, though, he took it upon himself to open her door and escort her into the Hawk & Hound Pub.

The place hadn't changed much since she'd last seen it. With its dark wood paneling and a roaring fire in the corner pot-bellied stove, the restaurant sported a rustic charm, and great pub food—both of which earned loyal, repeat customers. She did notice a few extra tables packed into the rectangular dining room, all occupied.

"I doubt we'll get a seat."

"Don't worry. I made reservations." He signaled to one of the waitresses, who grabbed a couple of menus, and then led them to a raised bistro-style table by the window. Zack helped Heather with her coat and hung it on the back of her chair. Always the gentleman, he waited for her to sit before taking his own seat.

As Heather placed her purse on the window ledge, she thought she heard her cell phone beep, but it was hard to tell over the crowd. "Do you mind terribly, if I check my messages? It could be—"

"About Lottie? Certainly. Go ahead."

She breathed a thank you and pulled the device from her bag. When she read the message, her chest collapsed, as if all the air had been sucked from the room. For a split-second, she felt like throwing the cell across the room, but it wasn't the phone's fault. If she hadn't been in public, and with the tear-fearing Zack, she would have burst out crying. As it was, she simply stuffed the cell back in her bag. Thankfully, the waitress arrived with their beers. Heather could stand a shot of alcohol.

"Are you okay? Is it Lottie?"

She shook her head. "My boss. He doesn't have any shifts for me. This week or next." In other words, *never*. "No doubt he heard of my arrest and doesn't want me around." Like the people in Kate's Kitchen. How could she have forgotten the reception she'd received there?

The whole town, *everyone*, was against her. Coming to the pub with Zack had been a mistake. She stood to leave. Zack reached for her hand.

"What's the hurry, then?"

"I'm not welcome here, Zack. I'm not welcome anywhere."

"That's not true. Look around."

She took in the room. No one smirked their disapproval. The few people who caught her eye nodded their acknowledgement and went back to their conversations in a leisurely fashion.

Heather sank into her chair. "You talked to them?"

"I met with my mom's friends—members of the Ladies' Auxiliary. I told them you're innocent." He gazed about the room. "They spread the word."

Thankful, she leaned across the table and kissed his cheek. "You've got a lot of clout in this town, Zack Jones."

He bowed his head, looking both appreciative and modest. "People trust me. Plus, I helped put out the fire you're accused of setting. They probably think I have some inside knowledge—a concrete reason to believe in you."

"You don't, though."

"Sure I do. I have your promise. You told me you're innocent. Right?"

"Right."

"That has to be enough." He held her hand, palm to palm. "But you need more to see you through, so I got you a little something."

"A *Get Out of Jail Free* card?"

He chuckled. "No. But I hope it will be almost as useful."

Zack reached into his shirt pocket with his other hand and pulled out a keychain with a beautiful, shiny rock inside. "It's a moonstone. It's supposed to bring you luck."

"Thanks, Zack." She clipped it to her purse. "That's really sweet of you."

"I wish I'd given it to you before you got that message from your boss."

"Bad timing all around."

Heather rested her chin on her fist—her head and heart heavy. She had no idea how she'd support Lottie or pay her bills. And it was so close to Christmas.

"I don't want to see that worried look," Zack said, practically nose to nose with her. "We'll figure out everything. I guarantee it."

She let her gaze slip from his eyes to his mouth, to read his lips over the room's noise. Heather remembered the taste of those lips, the thrill of his kisses—both commanding and gentle. And the way nothing else in the world had mattered on that lone night she'd spent in his arms.

She closed her eyes, anticipating another kiss. Maybe her luck *was* changing.

"I think the whole town's here tonight," an unfamiliar voice interjected, shattering the moment.

She turned. A tall, ruggedly attractive man, with dark hair and green eyes stood next to the table. Her date offered a smile—a pained one. Had Zack wanted to share a kiss, too? Only to be prevented by the newcomer's arrival?

"Heather, this is our fire chief, Ian King."

"Sorry to interrupt," Ian said, his face flushed. "I saw you from across the room and wanted to remind you about my cousin's wedding. You're still planning to bartend—right, Schwartz?"

"Definitely."

Relief smoothed Ian's brow. "Great. If only we could find a few more servers.

"Heather's looking for a job."

Ian scrutinized her. By now, he had to know she was the one accused of setting the fire under his watch. There was no way he'd hire her to serve tables at his cousin's wedding. Unless he hated his cousin.

"Are you free two Saturdays from now? If you are, you've got a job."

Maybe he hadn't heard about her troubles, after all. "Thanks. But I'm the one suspected of—"

Ian placed his hands on the table and leaned in. "Zack believes you're innocent, and he's a pretty good judge of character. That works for me. I'll let him fill you in on the details."

"Would you care to join us?" Zack offered, raising his beer.

"No, thanks. You seemed kind of busy before I stopped by. I'll leave you to it." He gave them a quick nod and found a lone chair in the opposite corner.

"Busy?" Zack cupped her shoulder. "Remind me…what we were doing?"

She wet her lips and imagined his mouth on hers. *Heavenly.*

Then she clutched the table, using it as an anchor to keep herself from leaping over to his side and kissing him senseless. "As Ian said, the whole town is here. You want them gossiping about us, *Schwartz?* Why did he call you that?"

"A nickname. Short for...uh..."

"Spill it."

"Schwarzenegger."

He laughed and she joined in. The name suited him. At least, as far as his build went. His accent and politics were completely different.

"Got a secret love child you want to tell me about?"

"Any kid of mine wouldn't be a secret. I'd proudly tell the world about him—or her—whether I was married to the mother or not. I wouldn't care what anyone thought."

She shook her head. "You care a lot about people. You wouldn't fight fires...wouldn't risk your life for the community, if you didn't."

"I want to give back, yes. That doesn't mean I'm willing to let other people rule my life."

She wished she had his conviction. "I guess, in a way, I still let Chase control mine."

"You shouldn't. The man's bad news, and I know a thing or two about that. My father was the same. Used to hit my mom."

Heather hadn't suspected the abuse in Zack's family, but it offered an explanation for Zack's response to tears. Had he witnessed his mother's distress?

"My dad died when I was five," he told her. "But I can still remember how awful life was with him. Even as a boy, I tried to protect my mom and, one time, received a broken rib in return."

And as an adult, he'd taken a job as a bouncer. What would Dr. Phil say about that? Was Zack still trying to break up his parents' fights? Metaphorically?

"For years, me and my mom took care of each other," he continued. "We overcame the past and moved on." He held Heather's hand again. "You can, too."

She wondered how much Zack had actually moved on. Was he hardwired to respond to damsels in distress—to be their rescuer—just as he rescued people from burning buildings? If so, his interest in her could stem from her role as an abused spouse. A troubling thought. She'd prefer a man who liked her because of *who* she was, rather than *what* she was.

Thank goodness Ian had interrupted them before the kiss.

She had no time for a romance with Zack, anyway. A lot of desire for one, but she had other more pressing issues. Namely, her daughter, her freedom, and finding an employer who didn't watch the nightly news.

Maybe the Hawk & Hound needed more servers. Generally, Monday was an off-night in the restaurant business, but the place was packed and Heather counted only two waitresses. She was about to start collecting dirty dishes to help out, when she noticed Lily Parker and Garret Frost, the eldest of the Frost siblings, looking cozy together at a table close to the small stage.

Beside them sat Garret's parents—Harold and Sylvia. Then, through the door, came three more patrons—Erik Wedge, Joey Frost, and a man Zack identified as Noel Fletcher—all wearing their police uniforms.

How cozy.

Heather swiveled in her seat, turned her face toward the window to avoid looking at them. "It's so busy here tonight."

"With Billy Boy's closed, this pub is about the only place in town to get a beer," Zack explained. "Plus, I'm sure a lot of people are here to see the entertainment."

"Entertainment?"

The clattering of applause rose from the crowd. With it, Zack tilted his head toward the man stepping onto the stage.

Heather's breath caught as she recognized Jim Frost. Now she understood why every Frost on the planet was in the pub tonight. They'd come to hear Jim play…while she wanted to disappear.

She couldn't take back what she'd tried to do last Christmas. How she'd attempted to come between Jim and his one, true love.

Did the shame of it show on her face? Could everyone see it?

Fortunately, all eyes focused on Jim as he began his set, singing a couple of well-known folk songs and accompanying himself on the guitar, while his wife, April, gazed up at him adoringly.

A waitress brought Heather and Zack their food and fresh beers, while Jim moved from folk, to country, and on to soft rock. He finished with a rousing rendition of *Jingle Bells* and invited the audience to sing along with him.

Zack's eyes twinkled as he joined in, his off-key attempt making Heather smile, in spite of her discomfort.

Jim left the stage amidst thunderous clapping and loud whistles from the police table. Heather remembered a line from a classic cartoon. Time for her to make like Snagglepuss the lion and...*exit, stage right.*

She wiped her mouth and crumpled her paper napkin. "Sorry, but I need to call it a night."

Zack looked at her plate. "You've hardly touched your burger."

"Between the beer and the anxiety of the last few days, I've got a pounding headache." Not entirely a lie. The claustrophobia didn't help, either. Brought on by a roomful of Frosts.

Zack settled the bill, refusing Heather's offer to pay for her half. He helped her with her coat, and she hurried to the exit. Zack reached to open the door for her, but someone on the other side beat him to it. Yet another Frost—Spencer, this time—entered with a pretty woman on his arm.

"Did we miss the show?"

"Only the first set," Zack assured him. "We freed up a table for you."

Spence smiled and provided the introductions, presenting the amber-eyed Robin Redmond.

"I'm glad I ran into you, Heather. Can you come to my office tomorrow?"

"Is something wrong?" More wrong than usual?

Spencer's mouth formed a straight line. "A new development."

Heather's heart sank. "That doesn't sound good. Please tell me now, otherwise I'll be up all night worrying."

Spence gestured to the door and the four of them slipped outside so as not to be overheard. The lawyer cleared his throat.

"Another witness stepped forward."

Zack stared at Spence. How could anyone have seen Heather commit a crime she didn't do? Now *three* people stood against her.

"How is that possible?"

"I don't know, but we need to find an answer to that exact question before we go to trial."

Heather stiffened beside him. "Who's this new witness?"

"Merry Palmer."

Zack recognized the name. He remembered seeing the young, purple-haired woman around town; and seeing her nametag whenever he dropped into Book Marks. He'd always wondered about the spelling—Merry instead of Mary. Maybe she'd been a Christmas baby.

"I've never heard of her," Heather told them, her tone indignant. "I don't even know this woman. Why did she think it was me? And if she's so sure, why didn't she come forward sooner?"

"She works downtown," Spence explained. "Walks past Billy Boy's on her way home. Merry says she saw a blond woman loitering around the bar on the night of the fire, but didn't think anything of it at the time. It wasn't until you came in the store today that she put two and two together. She identified you from a photo line-up at the police station."

Either Heather's mug shot, or that picture from the bar, Zack guessed. The photo he'd once admired was fast becoming her downfall.

Along with those gold, hoop earrings...

"At least *she* didn't identify your car and license plate," the lawyer continued.

Which meant Connor had? News to Zack. Heather hadn't mentioned that part of the evidence to him.

She covered her cheeks with her gloved hands. "I don't understand why this is happening."

Zack wanted to hold her, comfort her, but his arms were dead-weights. Useless.

He finally found his voice. "We aren't going to solve anything standing here in the cold. What time do you want Heather at your office?"

"I have an opening at ten. Does that work for you?"

Heather didn't answer, just kept shaking her head, muttering, "I'm innocent."

Zack agreed to the appointment on her behalf, and then whisked her away. They didn't talk on the drive to Ruth's. What was there to say?

After he saw Heather safely inside, he returned to his truck. On the trip home, he mulled over the new information, recalling that old adage, 'Where there's smoke, there's fire.' Sadly fitting, in this case.

He didn't trust Connor. Not at all. Zack was sure the kid was up to no good and had somehow coerced his grandmother into backing his statement. But that was before he'd heard about Connor spotting Heather's car.

And how did Merry fit into the mix?

As far as Zack knew, she didn't hang out with Connor. And, in spite of her wild hair, she seemed sweet, naive. He couldn't imagine why she'd lie about Heather. Someone she didn't even know.

As the evidence against Heather grew, he had to wonder if her troubles were brought about by plain bad luck? Or something else? And all that ruminating led him to a more disturbing question. One he couldn't get out of his head.

Was Heather as innocent as she claimed?

That night, Heather tossed and turned, finally jerking awake when she heard screaming. Beside her Lottie wailed like a horror movie heroine.

"It's okay, honey." Heather flicked on the light and took her daughter into her arms, the little girl's body rigid with fear.

"It's okay. Mommy's here."

As Lottie's screams faded to whimpers, a knock sounded on the door. Ruth poked her nose into the bedroom.

"Everything all right? Need my help?"

"We'll be okay. Sorry to wake you."

"I was on my way to the kitchen for a glass of water."

An obvious white lie, one Heather appreciated. Ruth could have used her en suite bathroom to get a drink.

A sympathetic smile brushed Ruth's lips as she closed the door, leaving Heather alone to soothe her child.

"Everything's fine, my sweet. Mommy will protect you."

As soon as she said the words, she frowned. Why should Lottie believe her? Heather hadn't protected her in the past. She'd allowed Chase's violence to creep into her child's life. Let it become a dark spectre. By enduring his treatment all those years.

What kind of a message did that send to her little girl?

Heather cuddled her daughter until Lottie's small body relaxed, until her eyes closed. Satisfied that Lottie was finally asleep, Heather slipped out of bed and went to her purse. She fished out

Juliette Armstrong's business card and put it by her cell phone, ready for the next morning.

She thought about the forty dollars in her wallet. Not a lot to offer a trained psychologist. Unfortunately, there wasn't much more in Heather's bank account—the amount dwindling each day she spent out of work.

Despite the warmer reception she'd received from the folks in the pub, her chances of getting a job in town were bleak. After all the news coverage, would Burlington be any better?

Feverish from her racing thoughts, Heather padded down the hallway to the front door and opened it just enough to poke her head into the cool darkness outside. Her breath formed ghost-like clouds in the pre-dawn air, and the streetlamps cast soft arcs of light making the snow glisten against the shadowy surrounds.

She opened the door a little wider and heard a soft thump. She glanced down. In moving the door, she'd knocked over a small, rectangular box, which now lay on its side.

Heather checked the street. Not a soul in sight. Whoever left the package was long gone.

She turned her attention back to the box. The way her week was going, Heather wondered if it contained a bomb.

Chastising herself for such gruesome thoughts, she reached out, picked up the surprisingly weightless package and brought it inside, locking up behind her.

In the quiet kitchen, she turned on the lights. Lottie's name was printed across the brown wrapping. No address, no stamps.

A sudden chill raised the hairs on Heather's neck. Who would leave a package for Lottie? What if one of the hateful town gossips had sent something to scare her?

Curiosity overriding caution, Heather pulled the scissors from the knife block set on the counter, snipped the wrapping, and slowly opened the cardboard box inside, her eyes widening at the contents…a teddy bear, slightly larger than her hand. The furry critter wore Christmas pajamas—reindeer running across a blue background.

Who would leave a present for Lottie? Zack?

Heather checked the box. Nothing inside gave a hint about the sender. The printed letters on the wrapper, didn't look familiar, which meant anyone could have sent the bear to her daughter.

"Great," Heather said, with a sigh. "One more mystery to solve."

At least this time, it was a cute one.

CHAPTER TEN

The next day, after her appointment with Spence, Heather and Lottie took a bus back home—despite protests from Ruth and Wenda, who wanted them to stay.

Actually, they wanted *Lottie* to stay.

Heather appreciated the offer, but it was past time for her and Lottie to return to their normal routine. At their own home. So Heather spent the rest of the week driving between appointments in Carol Falls and their apartment in Burlington, where Lottie caught up at school.

Heather worried about the extra mileage and the cost of running her gas guzzler to and fro, but it couldn't be helped. Their life was in Burlington, while the answers to her problems lay in Carol Falls.

Friday night they stayed over at Ruth's and, Saturday morning, Heather took Lottie to her rehearsal. She spotted Zack there, showing the children more magic tricks.

Her heart leapt around in her chest at the sight of him, in spite of the fact they hadn't really connected since their date at the Hawk & Hound.

Except for a game of phone tag. And Heather feared his calls sprang from his need to keep tabs on her because of the bail money more than any real concern.

She could hardly blame him for losing confidence in her, now that Ms. Palmer had stepped forward. Yet his absence from her life had created a hollowness, a void that all the busyness of the week couldn't fill. She missed his support, his smile and, seeing him now—in that body-hugging red sweater, the color of which made his eyes a darker chocolate—had her daydreaming about what magic tricks he could perform for her...in private.

Luckily, she had her child there to distract her. Lottie was far too reserved to approach Zack, but watched his every move. Same as her mother. Only Heather was mesmerized for an entirely different reason. When the kids broke off into their rehearsal groups, Zack finally approached Heather.

"How'd the meeting with your lawyer go?"

Really? That was his opening line? No explanation of where he'd been all week?

Heather quelled her frustrations. "Spence didn't have much to add from what he'd told us at the pub."

"Any plans today?"

She gave him a slant-eyed look. "Thought I'd tweak my résumé and apply for jobs online. Then I'm picking Lottie up at five."

"We need to talk."

Ominous words. They wore at the grain of hope she'd held on to for them—as friends, at least. Maybe he really was giving up on her completely. But why not say so—here and now?

"I promise to have you back in time for Lottie," he coaxed.

Did he have a new lead? One he didn't want to share in public? Was that the reason for his guardedness? She could stand there asking silent questions all day. Or she could go with him and get the answers.

They got in his truck, crossed the covered bridge and headed out of town. Heather gripped the armrest.

"What did you want to tell me?"

"There's something I want to show you, first. We can talk there."

"A *mystery* destination?" A fitting locale for the theme of her life, right now.

"Somewhere we can unwind and discuss your case in private. It's a little over an hour away. Is that okay?"

Lottie was occupied for the day, both Ruth and Wenda were on hand—what could go wrong? Heather sent the adults a quick text message to let them know she was only a phone call away.

That done, she leaned back in her seat. Not that she could completely relax in Zack's presence. For one, she wanted to hear the news he seemed hesitant to share. For two, three, four and the rest, she tried to make her eyes behave, but her gaze always strayed. It slid over his chest, as she imagined him without the jacket and sweater, exactly as he was on that night so long ago when they were skin to skin. And when he spoke, she was a goner. The low timbre of his voice rumbled over her, through her, jangling her senses.

She thought back to their first meeting, how their friendship had blossomed within the walls of Billy Boy's. Now they spent most of their time confined together in the cab of his truck. Or dining. What would Chase think about that? Her in the company of a guy who actually encouraged her to eat.

No. She didn't want to think about Chase. Not while she was with another man. She imagined writing her ex-husband's name on a blackboard, picking up the eraser and wiping the letters away—as she'd been coached.

She happily moved on to a safer topic. "Thanks for Lottie's bear."

"Bear?"

"You didn't leave her a plush one as a present? At Ruth's door?"

"Wish I'd thought of it. Should we be concerned?"

If he hadn't left it, who did? One of the gossips from the diner, perhaps? Were they trying to make amends by leaving a gift for her daughter? If so, would they even know where to find her?

"I don't think there's a problem. I checked the toy thoroughly before giving it to Lottie. Maybe it's from one of the other kids in the play." Heather doubted the explanation, even as she gave it. "Or one of Ruth's neighbors could have left it." That made more sense. Perhaps someone who didn't have grandchildren of her own to spoil.

Zack and Heather drove for about ninety minutes, warming into an easy chit-chat about the last movies they'd seen and which sports teams they favored. It felt like old times when they used to talk while she cashed out.

The tunes on Zack's radio, including a twangy version of *It's Beginning to Look a Lot Like Christmas,* filled in the quiet moments and provided an excellent soundtrack as they admired the passing trees—festively dressed with a layer of twinkling snow on their leafless branches.

He turned off the highway and they came to the village of Quechee, where they crossed another covered bridge built over an icy waterfall. Zack signaled left and left again, then nosed the truck into a parking spot beside a sprawling brick structure.

"This place used to be a mill. Now, they blow glass here."

Simon Pearce. Heather remembered reading about the lovely creations the artists made—in glass, pottery and wood.

"I hope you brought your appetite," he said, opening her door.

"They serve food here, too?"

"We'll eat first, then look around."

In the restaurant, a waitress led them to a table by one of the many large windows. Heather feasted on the view.

The cantilevered dining room jutted out, suspended over the river. Even at this time of year, the water flowed beneath them, over and under the built-up ice, surging its way to the crescent-shaped falls and tumbling onto the rocks below with abandon, before calmly making its way under the covered bridge.

"So beautiful." She turned to Zack, to see if he agreed, but he was looking at her.

Only her.

"Very beautiful."

She dipped her head to hide the warmth in her cheeks. A week ago, she would have brushed off the compliment and added a self-deprecating remark. She fought against the old habit and basked in his praise, while thanking providence she'd worn appropriate clothing, this time—a sleek, tan pantsuit with a teal blouse. Dressing well made her feel better about herself.

"I thought maybe you'd given up on me."

He didn't answer. When she lifted her head, she found him staring out the window, his jaw clenched.

"I have to admit, when I heard there was another witness, it shook me—that and discovering Connor identified your car."

She thought she'd told Zack everything. Had she forgotten to mention that specific point of evidence when they met over breakfast at Kate's? "I was exhausted...overwhelmed. It's surprising I can remember my own name anymore. If that one omission is a deal breaker for you, let's get out of here now."

Before she could rise from her chair, Zack grasped her hand. "I needed some time to think—not only about the Trivetts and Merry, but about the fire itself. It made me realize something."

The waitress brought them water and menus, pre-empting the

rest of Zack's explanation. Once they were alone again, he continued.

"Remember how we thought someone set the fire to cover the robbery?"

"Yes. But the fire actually drew attention to the theft."

"Exactly. If you'd taken the money, you'd have slipped in and out unnoticed with that key from your jewelry box. Arson would be the last thing on your mind. Since the crimes are obviously connected, if you didn't do one, you couldn't have committed the other. And your car? You've been driving that old bucket for years. Someone could have described it to Connor."

"So you believe me. Believe in my innocence."

"Nothing else makes sense."

She wished his faith in her came from the heart, but she'd take logic, for now. "Where does that leave us?"

"I said I'd help you with these charges—figure out who committed the crimes."

"Difficult when the police have tied our hands."

"But not impossible. The truth is important to me, and I mean to find it. So I made it my goal to talk to all of Billy's staff this week."

"You went to their houses?"

"Didn't have to. You hang out at Kate's Kitchen long enough, you bump into everyone in Carol Falls."

Heather's insides melted. He hadn't abandoned her. He'd been working on his own to help her. How typically Zack.

"Joey and Fletch cautioned you about questioning people. I don't want you getting into trouble because of me."

"I didn't ask a blessed thing. I let our bar comrades do the talking."

"And?"

"All of them seem genuinely shocked by your arrest. They believe in your innocence."

"That's reassuring." Knowing others were behind her brought warmth to her chest, her soul. But Zack's support meant the most of all. "Did you spend all week at Kate's?"

"No. I also picked up a few days working a contract with Jim Frost."

She hoped her voice wouldn't betray her apprehension. "How

did that go?"

"Jim pays well but, more important, he's working on the house where Mrs. Trivett and her grandson are staying. I wanted an opportunity to question Connor."

"Did you?"

"He avoided me, for the most part. Acted nervous the rest of the time. There's definitely something up with that boy."

"What about Mrs. Trivett? Is she feeling better?"

"Yup. She's on the mend."

The waitress appeared again and took their orders. Before long, a plate bearing steak frites sat before Zack, while Heather opted for something more substantial than her usual garden salad, and chose the salmon.

"Tell me about that earring," Zack said, after his first couple of bites. "How long ago did you lose it? And where?"

"Don't know," she said around a mouthful of food. The lemon herb sauce was to die for. And the grilled asparagus…she'd definitely landed in culinary heaven. She sampled a bit more then said, "I lost the earring eight months ago, at least. I was running all over at the time—working, moving apartments, trying to get custody of Lottie, visiting her at Fern's, storing boxes at Ruth's. I didn't notice it was missing until a co-worker mentioned I was wearing only one."

"Mmmmm. Maybe I've read too many detective novels—" he confessed "—and this may seem out of left field but…what if the arsonist wanted to look like you?"

"You mean a case of mistaken identity? Like Spence suggested?"

"No. I'm talking about someone deliberately impersonating you. What if someone stole your earring a year ago to use at some point in the future…to get you in trouble?"

A chill crept through her body and settled in her bones. She could think of only one person who'd want to intentionally harm her.

"What do you think? Is my idea totally off the wall?"

"It's out there," she admitted. "But I sure feel better knowing I have your support."

His eyes widened. "You're pretty calm about all this."

"I'm working on it. With Juliette's help."

"Juliette?"

"Dr. Armstrong. I've been seeing her. Professionally."

"To deal with the charges?"

"Really, it's to help my daughter. Most days, Lottie has come along for the sessions. I want her to grow up to be a strong, independent woman—to confront her fears. Which means I have to battle mine first. I need to be that strong woman for her. To lead by example."

She imagined Chase's criticism, hearing him say, 'Therapy costs money.' Anything she'd ever wanted was expensive and foolish.

Heather shook the thought away and reminded herself she was talking to Zack, not her ex. "I worked out a barter system with Juliette, offered to clean her house in exchange for the sessions. She wasn't interested—said she'd already hired Mrs. Belmont to help her with that—but she really needed someone to clean up her receipts. When I mentioned I used to be a bookkeeper, Juliette leapt on it."

Zack took a sip of water. Then another. The tension of his silence closed around Heather, cementing her shoulders in place.

"That's good, Heather. I'm glad you're getting what you need from someone."

The words were right, despite Zack's tight-lipped delivery. She'd thought he'd be pleased for her. After all, he'd suggested she contact Juliette in the first place.

It had taken a lot of courage to admit she needed help. To actually pursue it. No matter how many celebrities talked about getting therapy, no matter how many regular people appeared on TV shows seeking advice from trained psychologists, there was still a stigma attached to it.

Or was Zack upset because she'd reached out to someone else, instead of him?

"If you're in Carol Falls tomorrow, maybe we can do some therapy that's a little more fun—a sleigh ride at Frost Farms."

Inside, Heather cringed, but quickly plastered a big grin on her face. There were some fears she'd still rather avoid. "Lottie would love that. But I can't tomorrow. There's something I need to do."

"Anything I can help with?"

"No." She blotted her mouth with the napkin, gearing up for her big announcement. "I'm going to the penitentiary. I've spent all week preparing myself to see Chase."

She was on his visitors' list. He'd made it clear he wanted her to keep him posted on Lottie. Heather feared his request had more to do with maintaining a tight grip on the woman who'd dared to divorce him. Either way, she'd never gone to see him. Never worked up the nerve.

"I think it's a bad idea."

"Why?"

"You're out on bail. Should you associate with a convict?"

"I already cleared it through Spence."

"Okay...but after what your ex did to you, I'd be giving him a wide berth."

"Really? I think if someone hurt *you*, you'd confront them."

"That's different. I'm a guy. I can handle myself."

Unless crying was involved. Then he'd run for the hills.

"I may not be able to compete in a physical fight like you, but I'm talking about something else. About overcoming my fear of Chase. For my sake...and for Lottie's."

He tilted his head from side to side, as if weighing the argument.

"It's something I need to do in order to heal. Also, it's the only lead we can pursue."

She couldn't go back to feeling numb again. Couldn't go on playing the stoic and pretend everything was fine, when it wasn't—the way she had when they'd first met. But the tears and anxiety weren't working for her, either. If she could get her emotions under control, and Zack could confront his difficulties with witnessing those kinds of feelings, maybe they'd have a chance together. As more than friends.

"You think Chase is behind this? That he framed you?"

"It's the one explanation that makes sense."

"And you think he'll actually admit it?"

"He always bragged about his intelligence. If Chase is at the center of this, he won't be able to stop himself from tooting his own horn."

Zack leaned back in his chair, working his jaw as he mulled it over. "You'll be going through some lonely rural areas and that old car of yours could conk out on you anytime. Why don't you take my truck? Better yet, why don't I drive you there myself?"

That sort of defeated the point of her confronting Chase alone, didn't it? The idea of Zack coming with her, though, at least as far as the prison's parking lot, was very reassuring. "That would be great, Zack."

"It's a date then. And so is this. Don't even think about opening your purse."

A date? Though the setting was romantic, their conversation certainly hadn't strayed far beyond business. Not surprising. Until her case was closed, she couldn't expect more from him. No matter how much she might wish for it.

She thanked him as he paid the bill. Fern had taken her to some ritzy places in New York, but none of them compared to this restaurant—both in atmosphere and food. She'd gobbled up every bit of her meal and practically licked the plate.

Though, she had to admit, the presence of a particular delectable firefighter certainly added to her overall enjoyment.

They went into the gallery, decorated like a Martha Stewart dream. Display tables, set as if for dinner, sported red placemats, elegant wineglasses, and sprigs of holly berries curled around gold plates. Glass pears, apples and teardrop baubles glistened as they dangled from red ribbons on Christmas trees. There were even silver and glass menorahs for Chanukah.

After taking it all in, Zack took her hand and led the way to the lower level, where artisans worked in teams of two to create the beautiful goblets they'd seen in the showroom. One man appeared with a glob of two thousand degree glass on a metal stick—a Merlin, holding a magic wand with a glowing orb at one end. He passed the glass onto the second artist, who then used his blowpipe to shape the ball into a form. The two craftsmen moved together as in a dance, their timing and precision perfect.

With the furnaces at full blast, the temperature in the basement rose to that of a scorching summer's day. Overheated, she and Zack slipped out the back door onto a small balcony that overlooked the falls.

Heather watched the rush of icy water below her, feeling more grounded than she had in years. Like the glassmakers inside, she was on a journey to create something new—gathering together the sands of her old existence and, with Juliette's help, reforming them into a better way of living.

Without fear. As free as the breeze that played through Zack's hair.

The light wind caressed the strands—invisible fingers tousling his curls. Heather wondered how it would feel to reach up and weave her own hands through his dark hair.

To touch. To take what she wanted. In spite of all the troubles around them.

He looked at her and smiled, one of those heart-throbbing smiles of his. One that told her he sensed what she'd been thinking. Thought it, too.

He drew her close, her fantasy coming to life. Only it was *his* fingers tangling her hair, *his* hands guiding her lips to his.

It was everything she remembered. *More*. When he deepened the kiss, she opened to him, felt the thrill of it down to her toes.

Vaguely, she heard more people join them on the platform. She should pull away. Tell Zack the timing was all wrong. That they needed to put their attraction on hold until all her issues were resolved. But she'd waited too long for this—to feel safe in a good man's arms, to feel the tingle of passion again.

A loud thump broke them apart. A collective gasp went through the spectators.

Heather followed the outstretched arm of one woman and saw a bird—a sparrow—on the cement balcony. Unmoving. The poor thing must have flown right into the window.

She turned to Zack, but he was already in motion. While everyone else stood gawking, he bent down and scooped up the bird in his big, gloved hands.

"I think it's stunned. Maybe in shock." He opened his jacket and held the bird against his chest to keep it warm.

Standing beside him, Heather could see the sparrow blink, but that seemed to be the only thing it could manage.

The people on the deck held vigil, keeping their distance, probably guessing their approach would add to the creature's distress.

Heather lost track of how long they stood there. Possibly ten minutes, maybe more. Zack cupped his hands so the bird wouldn't feel trapped. Gradually its little head turned this way and that, taking in its surroundings. Still, it remained cradled in the protection Zack offered, soaking up the man's heat.

At last, the sparrow stretched its wings. In another minute, it hopped onto the railing, took a last glance at its savior and then flew off.

Everyone on the platform applauded Zack and his tiny patient. Heather clapped too, and kissed him again.

Such a great guy. Her *guy.*

As his arm curled around her, Heather's smile wilted. Zack was ever ready to come to the rescue. Did he view *her* as a wounded creature needing his help?

If that was the only reason he liked her, what would happen to his attraction once she triumphed over her problems and fears?

Would his affection for her fly away, too?

CHAPTER ELEVEN

Heather woke early the next day. Truth be told, between Lottie's restless dreams and her own night spectres, she'd barely slept. Every time she shut her eyes, a vision of Chase appeared. He'd start off being the man she'd first met—attractive, charismatic.

Then came the anger.

It had always been there. She knew that now. The way he'd slam his hand against the steering wheel when stuck in traffic. The way his face would harden with silent rage, whenever something didn't go his way.

Back when they were dating, those bouts ended quickly, and he'd crack a smile. Once they were married, he didn't bother to contain his temper. It would simmer to a boil, burning her in the process.

Heather swung her legs out from the sheets and sat on the edge of the bed. She didn't want to think about her ex anymore. Not when Zack was in her life…and taking up residence in her heart.

Still, images of Chase seeped into her dreams.

She'd never discussed the nightmares with her daughter. Never asked Lottie for details about hers. Feared they'd resemble her own.

Fortunately, in their counseling, Heather was learning the skills to deal with it all and exorcize her demons.

She drew her daughter into a hug and smoothed the sweat-dampened hair from Lottie's face. "Remember what Juliette told us. Next time, when the monster comes after you, don't run. Stand your ground and tell him to go away." Good advice. Heather hoped she'd remember it, today.

"I'm too afraid."

"We're all afraid of things, honey."

"Not Daddy. He's never scared."

"Daddy, too." Perhaps he was the most fearful of all and that's why he lashed out. "Remember, it's only a dream. It can't hurt you."

Lottie's brow creased. Heather kissed the spot, to ease her little girl's worries. "I know I didn't do such a good job of shielding you in the past. Especially from those fights Mommy and Daddy used to have. But, I promise you, those fights will never happen again. You have nothing to worry about. We're safe. Pinkie swear." They linked baby fingers, sealing the promise.

Heather helped Lottie get ready for the day and then turned her attention to her own attire. Through Ruth, who saw Chase regularly, she knew visitors had to adhere to a specific dress code. No sweats, no skirts, no dresses. No hats, no headbands or hoodies, and nothing that would resemble a uniform belonging to a law enforcement officer.

Heather chose gray dress pants and a cool mint sweater. She pulled her hair into a simple ponytail, then followed Lottie down the hall to the living room. The little girl hopped onto a dining room chair beside her aunt and peered at Wenda's latest sketch—a makeup design for the toy soldiers in the play.

Ruth emerged from the kitchen with a bowl of cereal for Lottie and gave Heather the once-over, nodding her approval. "You're all set. Now, don't worry about Lottie. We have a fun day planned for her at rehearsal."

The older woman wore a plain navy top and matching slacks. But the silk scarf around her neck really drew Heather's attention—with its hand-painted peach flowers.

A present from her sister, Fern. The year Heather turned thirty.

Ruth brought a hand to her throat. "I hope you don't mind. It really spruces up my outfit. Adds a bit of spring, don't you think?"

"Yes," Heather said, but her smile drooped. She tried to remember the last time she'd seen the scarf. She wouldn't have brought it with her on this trip—not in the dead of winter. Had Ruth picked it up the night of the arrest?

"I don't mind you borrowing my things but…"

Heather stopped herself, uncomfortable suggesting that Ruth

ask before taking. Sure, Heather contributed grocery money to the household, and she did a lot of the cooking whenever she visited, but she'd accepted Ruth's offer to stay here, rent free, during the upcoming week of evening rehearsals.

She'd originally made the arrangements so Lottie wouldn't get overtired with the drive back and forth to Burlington and had cleared the absence with Lottie's teacher, who organized extra homework for her daughter to do during the week before the Christmas break.

Little did Heather know her car would finally give up the ghost, yesterday, after a quick trip to the Cross Roads Market for a carton of milk. The clunker sputtered and coughed its way back, finally conking out a block from Ruth's house—stranding Heather and Lottie in Carol Falls.

Luckily, Ruth and Wenda welcomed them to stay as long as needed. Plus, the two loved Lottie and were always happy to babysit. What was a little scarf compared to that kind of support?

Still…

"If you want to borrow something of mine, I'd appreciate you checking with me first. That scarf was a gift from my sister, and I don't lend it to anyone."

Ruth stared at her, mouth agape, but she dutifully unwrapped the silk from her neck and placed it in Heather's outstretched hand.

Heather slipped the scarf around her own neck, tugged on her boots and grabbed her coat. "I'll be three or four hours."

"Take your time. We love having Lottie to ourselves."

Such statements used to make Heather happy. To her, it meant Lottie was well-loved by her extended family. Today, after the scarf business, Ruth's tone was terse, but the older woman smiled sweetly, as always.

Heather heard a knock and pulled back the front door. There stood Zack, wearing a thick, red and black lumberjack shirt under his jacket.

"Perfect timing," she told him.

"I aim to please."

Please, he did. She caught a whiff of his cologne. The woodsy stuff made her head spin. Or was that from the sight of him—big and solid—standing tall, as if nothing could hold him back, or get in his way.

They climbed into his truck and headed out of town, country music playing low on the radio. As one singer crooned about his four by four, Heather told Zack about her car woes, and thanked him again for driving today. He promised to take a look at her vehicle and see if he could fix it himself to avoid the cost of a mechanic.

Was there no end to the man's talents?

They held hands whenever Zack didn't need both of his to navigate the roads, which curved around rivers and hills. The rest of the time Heather rested her hand on his muscled thigh. Touching him there felt bold, intimate—*right*. His strength reassured her more than she could say.

A few small towns sprung up along the way, but mostly they saw snow-covered farms. Many had kiosks built near the road. Heather imagined, come summer, the farmers would be out selling their crops from these booths—apples, maple syrup, cheese.

Zack had described the area as lonely, but Heather had never thought of the rural areas around Carol Falls that way. Not with the Green Mountains as a backdrop. To her, the place was clean, fresh, open and colorful—especially in autumn when the trees wore vibrant shades of yellow, orange and red—and stretched out for miles. A world she missed since living in the city.

The terrain changed as they approached the prison...a dense forest closing in on them. Finally, the tall, razor-wire fence appeared through the trees, coiling snake-like around the drab, industrial-style building.

Following her directions, Zack pulled into the prison parking lot and turned off the ignition. She remained in her seat, unable to make her feet move. Silly to drive so far and chicken out now.

"You want me to come in with you?"

"I don't know if they'll even let you into the waiting room, since you're not on the visitors' list."

They sat in silence, the heat from the vehicle dissipating until Heather could see the white mist of her breath.

"I wish I could be there for you."

"Me, too." With trembling fingers, Heather buttoned the top of her coat. "But I have to do this on my own."

She got out of the car, her legs shaking so badly it was difficult to walk. She clutched the moonstone keychain Zack had given her.

For luck.

"Keep moving," she told herself. "One step at a time."

Heather made it to the entrance and joined the line of visitors, ID in hand. The heavy, steel door clanged shut behind her, making her jump. She'd been in prison before—in the Carol Falls' jail, and in the confines of her marriage. Still, in this correctional center, she could almost taste the oppression, feel the weight of hopelessness heavy on her chest.

She put her personal belongings in a locker and then went through security. It resembled an airport checkpoint, with a metal detector and a physical search. When the female guard patted her down, Heather flashed back to her own arrest—the violation, the humiliation.

She took a number and went into the waiting lounge that contained a vending machine for snacks and a coffee counter. Though the aroma reminded her she'd skipped breakfast, she wasn't about to consume anything. Her stomach was churning enough already.

Her hands were cold one minute, clammy the next, and she wiped them on her pant legs. Another officer brought a dog around to sniff for drugs. She would have liked to pet the animal to calm her nerves, but didn't dare try.

She glanced at the other visitors—adults with strained smiles, speaking quietly to their teenaged children, who slumped in their seats, their angst visible through the veneer of boredom. The sparkling Christmas tree in the corner did little to cheer anyone. Instead, it added to the general despair. There'd be no merry Christmas for the loved ones of the men incarcerated here.

"Fifty-six."

Her number. She stood...followed a third guard down a hall with doors along the side. Due to the nature of Chase's crime and because she was considered his victim, the guard led her to a no-contact area for the visit. She'd seen the same kind of room in movies, where a sheet of Plexiglas down the middle kept the inmate separate from the visitor. The small barrier didn't ease Heather's anxiety. Chase had the ability to reduce her to ashes with a look or a casual insult.

He still owned her. Owned her fear.

She sat...stared at the empty chair on the other side. She'd braced herself to see him right away. Had he planned to keep her waiting? To show her he still held the power in their relationship? To put her on edge?

The prisoners' door clicked and opened. A man appeared and took his seat opposite her. A man much altered—older, paler, his cocky smirk turned bitter. She'd once thought him handsome. After a few beatings, her idea of male beauty changed.

He'd always dressed well, careful to keep up appearances, especially his own. Or was it a case of concealment? Had he covered up his ugly side by choosing nice clothes?

Now, he wore the standard jumpsuit and yet managed to look even more intimidating than he had in designer threads.

She avoided his eyes, remembering the coldness in them. For Chase, direct eye contact was a challenge, so she'd learned to look down, to show her submission. Would that ingrained response ever go away?

He puffed out his chest and angled closer to the palm-sized disk in the middle of the glass, through which they could communicate.

"You finally showed up. Feeling generous at Christmas?"

Heather wrapped her arms around herself, hoping to contain the wild beating of her heart. Perspiration stung her upper lip, but she didn't dare wipe it away. Didn't want him to know he'd already gotten to her. She refocused and, raising her chin, launched into the script she'd prepared. "I came to talk to you about a fire in Carol Falls."

"Not about our daughter? Classic. You shut me away and won't bring her to visit."

"Prison is no place for a little girl." *Damn.* She'd promised herself she wouldn't respond to his taunts.

"It's no place for anyone. But here I am."

Lottie could decide about visits herself in a couple of years. Until then...

"Your mother keeps you well informed about our daughter." Before he could respond, she segued into her practiced lines. "I'm here for an entirely different reason. I came to—"

"Perform your wifely duties?"

He dragged his tongue over his lips and she almost gagged. The thought of him kissing her, touching her, held no pleasure. Only pain. She shivered with revulsion.

"You cold, baby doll?"

She clasped her shaking hands together and held them in her lap—where he couldn't see them. "I came to talk to you about revenge. How far would you go to get it?"

"I heard you were arrested." He chuckled. "Couldn't have happened to a more deserving person, if you ask me. I'd give anything to see you locked up. That would be the perfect Christmas present." Chase gestured to his surroundings, his expression one of mock innocence. "Sadly, I'm not in a position to execute such a diabolical plan."

True. It didn't stop someone else from doing it on his behalf, however. And Heather doubted he'd willingly divulge *who*. Certain she couldn't learn anything else, she stood.

"Where are you going? We've only started."

She didn't answer. Instead, she turned her back to him and made her way to the door.

"Sit down. I'm not done with you, yet."

Heather froze. Instinct told her to do as he commanded—anything to avoid his punishment.

"You heard me, woman."

She ordered her knees to stop knocking. For now, a sheet of glass divided them. He couldn't hurt her.

"Don't you ever turn your back on me, bitch. You're the reason I'm here."

Slowly, she turned to face him. She leaned over the chair, placed her hands on the small ledge on her side of the Plexiglas, and looked him straight in the eyes.

"No, Chase. *You* are the reason you're here."

CHAPTER TWELVE

Heather was halfway across the parking lot before she realized it.

A light snow was falling around her, and the bleak surroundings looked softer, prettier. She stretched out her palm and captured a flake on her gloved hand.

She thought about catching another on her tongue, wondered if she'd look silly, and did it anyway. She ran the rest of the way to Zack's truck, saw him standing outside of it, and jumped into his open arms, laughing.

Zack had never seen her so genuinely happy. "Did Chase confess?"

"No. But confronting him was good—like Juliette said. I needed to face him again to move on with my life."

Zack figured it was good news for him, too. Even though Heather had divorced her husband, she hadn't really been emotionally free.

Not until now.

He held her, brushed a kiss against her temple. When she didn't pull away, Zack snuggled closer, and his heart banged a little harder in response.

He could have stayed that way for the next hour, holding her. But it was the middle of December and damn cold—in spite of the heat they always managed to generate when they touched. He sure didn't want his lady getting pneumonia. He planned to make Heather feverish in a much more enjoyable way. Very, very soon.

Once he'd freed her from the threat of jail.

Zack helped her into the passenger seat of his truck and climbed behind the wheel. During the ride back, he thought about the evidence they knew so far.

What had they missed?

"Maybe we're going about this the wrong way," he suggested. "Other than Chase, who would profit by framing you?"

"I have no idea. Maybe it's a case of mistaken identity, after all."

"What if it isn't? What if someone wants you out of the way?"

"Of what?"

He turned on the wipers and sent snow flying off the windshield. "Are you in line for an inheritance?"

"I might get something from my parents' estate, but they've practically disowned me. And they're in perfect health, according to Fern. She fills me in on their news."

He drove a few miles, rehashing the facts in his mind. "What about a payback? Have you upset anyone recently? Say in the past year?"

She looked so serious, he fumbled for a joke to make her smile. "How about a high school crush? One of those nerdy physicist-types you overlooked in the hall, who wants to make you so sick of planet Earth, you'll start a colony with him on Venus."

Heather grinned, the worry lines on her forehead softening. "Too hot there, and I'm prone to frizzies."

"Good to know. So, other than your smooth hair, what do you have of value? Got a treasure map stashed away somewhere?"

"Don't need one. I've got Lottie. She's my treasure."

The snow lifted and Zack could see the road much better. The case, too. Was Heather's daughter at the heart of this?

"If something happened to you, who would raise Lottie? Do you have it spelled out in a will?"

"I couldn't persuade Chase to go to a lawyer. Guess he doesn't plan on dying. You've made a good point, though. I need to check into a will for myself, now that I'm single again. Maybe I should get one of those Do-It-Yourself Kits."

"Or Spencer could help you with it. But, back to Lottie. Where would she live?"

"We always thought she'd be with Ruth," Heather replied, her tone matter-of-fact, as if the answer were obvious.

"And your testimony put Ruth's son behind bars."

Heather shook her head. "I see where you're going with this, but it couldn't be her. Ruth has complete access to Lottie. Visits anytime she wants. She doesn't need me out of the way. Besides, she's shorter than I am, and has an entirely different build. No one would mistake her for me. Even at a distance."

"What if she paid the witnesses to lie?"

"She's not rolling in dough."

"But Wenda is off to college soon, right? Does she have a scholarship, or what?

Heather wasn't sure. She didn't pry into Ruth's finances. "Wenda's marks are good, but they've never mentioned a scholarship."

"They would have, if she'd won one."

Did that mean her former in-laws had a secret supply of cash? Enough to bribe phony witnesses?

Heather stared out at the snow-covered landscape, the gloom of her situation creeping in again. She remembered Ruth's Christmas tree with Lottie's picture everywhere. And what had Ruth said today? 'We love having Lottie...*to ourselves.*'

Did Ruth view Lottie as her third child? And concoct a spiteful plan to claim her? Heather didn't want to believe it. But she couldn't ignore the possibility.

Back in Carol Falls, Zack drove Heather to the school.

While she went off to check on Lottie, a blur of kids whizzed past him in the hallway. The group sported headbands with fuzzy pink ears and long mouse tails attached to the seat of their pants. He laughed at their excited squeals.

Zack didn't have the acting bug. He hadn't been much for plays as a kid. Though, one year in elementary school, by virtue of his height, he scored the prize role of Robin Hood. He'd hated prancing around in tights, but he'd relished the sword fights and his shared kiss with Maid Marian.

Down the corridor, he spotted Duncan Frost, wearing a red tunic with big, yellow buttons. Two white crossbelts formed an X over his thin chest. His buddies, Nathan and Marcus, also dressed as toy soldiers, rushed behind him, their plumed hats off-kilter.

Pulling up the rear, the usually composed Sylvia Frost looked frazzled as the kids raced by her. "Duncan, we walk indoors. Remember?"

Garret's son slowed his pace—barely—and made a beeline for Zack. "Can you show us that card trick again? 'Cause you know what? Lottie wants to pick this time."

The boys stepped aside to reveal Heather's little girl hiding behind them, sparkling snowflakes painted on her face. Normally Zack would have encouraged the child to speak up for herself. In Lottie's case, he knew persuading her to come even this close to him was a huge leap forward.

He didn't approach her. Instead, he squatted down to her level, dug into his jacket pocket and retrieved his deck. After shuffling it, Zack fanned the cards and held them out to her.

She hesitated. A couple of feet separated them, but Zack didn't move. If she wanted to see the trick badly enough, she'd have to come to him.

With her friends' encouragement, Lottie took a tentative step. Then another. Slowly, she reached out and selected her card.

"Show it to your friends," Zack said, keeping his voice even. Difficult, because he really wanted to shout halleluiah, and high-five them all. "Make sure they see the card, but don't show it to me."

After the boys inspected it, Zack instructed Lottie to return the card. Then, with a little sleight of hand, Zack kept it on the top of the deck while making it appear he'd buried it in the middle of the stack. He grabbed a handkerchief from his other pocket and placed it around the deck, careful to keep Lottie's card loose and under the silk. He gave the cloth a wiggle, and her card fell out.

The children gasped in amazement. Nathan clapped. "Do it again."

Zack shuffled the deck for another round when, over their heads, movement caught his eye—Heather, in a corner, talking to a young woman.

He didn't recognize the new person. Rather, he recognized the sweater she wore—the same one Heather had given Ruth's daughter. Only then did he put two and two together. The young woman *was* Wenda.

Maybe she was trying to impersonate Marilyn Monroe, or some current popstar, but in that sweater and wearing a blond wig, she looked exactly like Heather.

Eerily so.

Heather must have seen the resemblance, too. She stood in front of Wenda, red blotches staining the cheeks of her otherwise pale face.

"Another time, guys," Zack replied, rising to his feet. "We better go help your mom, Lottie."

He held out his hand to the little girl, but she didn't take it. She did follow him when he headed toward Heather, though.

As the two of them neared, Ruth joined the heated debate, her voice strident. "From now on, Heather, you're not welcome in my house. My granddaughter, yes. Lottie's welcome anytime. But you need to collect your things today and get out."

Ruth and Wenda stormed off, leaving Heather gaping. Zack ran the rest of the way to her. "What did you say to them?"

Heather hugged a teary-eyed Lottie before answering. "Basically, what we talked about in the car."

"You accused them of framing you?"

"I asked questions around it. I tried to be subtle, but they obviously got the message." Heather examined her boots. "Guess it's my day for confrontations."

Guilt hit Zack like a sharp pain between his shoulder blades. Still, he figured Heather was better off without her in-laws. The force of their reaction made him suspect them all the more.

"What are you going to do now?"

"Go back to Burlington. Find a job."

"What about the wedding gig here? It's a sure thing."

"Only for one day. I need to find something full-time so I can get my car fixed and drive Lottie to her dress rehearsals next week."

"I said I'd take a look at it for you. If it's past repairing…well…you wouldn't need a car at all, if you stayed in town." He scrambled for a housing solution. "How about Juliette? Maybe she could put you up."

"She's a psychologist, Zack. Not an innkeeper," Heather joked, obviously trying to ease the tension of the past few minutes. "Even though I'm sharing personal information with her, it's not as if she's a friend. I couldn't impose that way."

And, in leaving town, Heather wouldn't be able to continue the sessions she and Lottie needed.

"You could take my truck."

"That's really generous, Zack. But I'd feel terrible stranding you for a whole week. What if there was another fire and you had to get to the station fast?"

"I'd manage." Hell, he'd run the distance, if necessary. "There's got to be a way to make it work."

"Don't worry about it, Zack. It's not your problem."

"It feels like my problem. I put those ideas in your head."

"I'm the one who acted. It's up to me to sort it out." She gave him a peck on the cheek—friend to friend. "I'll find a solution. I always do."

She grasped Lottie's hand and walked to the exit.

What were the chances of them solving the case with her living miles away? Or of them working out this thing between them?

"Wait." He caught up to the duo. "A few minutes ago, Lottie helped me with a magic trick. Came up to me and took a card out of my hand."

Heather's eyes misted. "She *did?*"

"Whatever you're doing—between the sessions with Juliette and the theater stuff—it's working. If you're thinking of pulling Lottie out of the show—"

"I wouldn't dream of it." She kissed the top of her daughter's head. "Maybe I could arrange for Lottie to leave dress rehearsals early, so we could take the last bus back to Burlington. On the performance night she'll have to stay until the end of the show for her final appearance, but I'll come up with an alternative by then."

"I've got an alternative right now. You can stay with me."

As soon as the invitation was out of his mouth, he had second thoughts. His house was small and the extra bedroom held his universal gym. The place was clean enough, but it wasn't set up for guests.

Especially when one of them was a shy little girl who mistrusted men.

"I truly appreciate your offer, Zack, but I don't think it's a good idea. Not without a chaperone," Heather added, blushing again.

"We have Lottie for that."

Heather frowned. She looked from him to Lottie and back to him again. Zack prepared himself for a *no.*

Just as well, really. No chaperone—especially not a pint-sized one—could keep him from the woman of his dreams. Certainly not in the close quarters of his home.

"We'll go to the hotel. It'll be…"

She moistened her lips, giving him a quick vision of a night alone with her at an exotic resort in the Bahamas, or the Caribbean.

"Easier," she tacked on, blasting his fantasy.

"Easier? At this time of year? Between the skiers and the out-of-towners coming for holiday dinners with relatives, you'll never get a room."

Someone hand me a shovel. He was digging himself in deeper every second.

"Well…if you're sure," Heather said, finally.

"I'm sure."

Sure that, while she was under his roof, he'd be condemned to a sentence of cold showers.

Heather knew Zack owned a little bungalow on the other side of town, but she'd never seen it.

At least, not in daylight.

From outside, it looked exactly as she expected. Sturdy, handsome—much like Zack, himself.

Entering the house, she scanned the living room. Short on knickknacks and big on comfort, the place sported a couch and recliner—both made of dark, padded leather. Taupe walls framed the other furnishings—a bookcase, dining table and chairs—all black with square lines. A huge, flat screen TV dominated one wall.

He gave them a tour of the rest of the house, taking them down the hallway and showing them the bathroom and how he'd set up his workout equipment in the spare room.

Zack stopped at the final door and opened it, revealing the place she remembered the most. The room with the king-size bed in it.

"You two can sleep here."

"What about you? I mean…where will you sleep?"

"On the couch."

Guilt niggled at her. "I feel terrible kicking you out of your bed."

"*I* feel terrible getting you kicked out of Ruth's."

"That wasn't your fault. I—"

He interrupted her apology with a kiss to her cheek. "Let's call it even."

Heather smiled. She liked the way he solved disagreements.

"I'll go pick up your stuff and tow your car here. Then I'll make us some dinner."

"You cook?" she asked, impressed.

"Don't get too excited. I only do the basics. Barbeques are my specialty."

"Not in the middle of winter."

"Best time." He grinned and disappeared out the front door to collect her belongings.

Ninety minutes later, they were seated around his dining table. He'd made steaks for the two of them and a hotdog with cheese for Lottie, who obviously enjoyed it, judging by the ketchup running down her chin. Her cry of, "Yum," confirmed it.

After dinner, and some homework, Zack found a Disney movie online. Halfway through the film, Lottie's head started to nod.

"I can carry her to the bedroom," Zack offered.

"I'd better do it."

Heather lifted her daughter, her back twinging in protest at the added weight. She looked forward to the day when the six-year-old didn't flinch around a guy.

With Lottie tucked in for the night, Heather returned to the living room to find a glass of red wine waiting for her. She picked it up from the coffee table and Zack raised his beer.

"Cheers."

"Thanks." She took a sip and tasted a hint of cherries. "Nice. Mellow."

"Good. I wasn't sure. My mom dropped off the bottle last Christmas. She says ladies prefer wine."

"I don't know if that applies to all ladies, but I certainly do."

She sighed and collapsed on the couch beside him. It had been a trying day. Sitting with Zack felt good, though. Not exactly comfortable—there was too much electricity between them for that. Too many tingles going through her when they accidentally brushed arms.

She fretted about her decision to stay with him. Particularly, if she couldn't shut down her libido. And that was next to impossible around Zack.

"Want to finish watching the movie?" she asked.

"We could. But I thought we'd watch it with Lottie tomorrow."

Thoughtful of him. What else could she use as a distraction? "Why don't you show me a trick? A *card* trick," she clarified, when he smirked.

Mischief flashed in his eyes. "You're blushing."

She slapped her hands against her cheeks. "Am I?"

"It's pretty."

"Really?"

"Very." He inched nearer.

"Last Christmas," she began, feeling another confession coming on. "When I left town…"

Zack shifted and faced the blank TV screen—his beer clutched between his big hands, his shoulders stiff.

"I hurt you." She realized that now. "I didn't mean to. I was so mixed up. So desperate to get Lottie back. I said—and did—things I wouldn't normally."

"Like make love to me."

His words carried such sorrow, her heart hurt. "I've never regretted it, Zack. You showed me how it could be with the right man. Sometimes, remembering that night with you is the only thing that gets me through the day. That memory…and having Lottie in my life."

"Is that so?"

How could he doubt it? "You must know how fabulous it was for me. How perfect you made it."

"I tried," he said, with a sexy grin. "But after you ran off—"

"I know it's a cliché, but honestly—it wasn't you, it was me."

He set down his beer and looped one arm over the back of the sofa. "Good to know. 'Cause I've always hoped for a repeat performance."

Zack took the glass from her hand and put it down beside his bottle. He leaned in—closer…closer.

Until their lips met.

The tingles she'd experienced when they'd brushed arms were nothing compared to this. Shivers quaked through her body.

Soon, his hands were in her hair, their tongues mating. When his fingers slid under her bra, she sighed, craving his touch more than her next breath.

Then reason clicked in. She couldn't make out with Zack in the middle of the living room. What if their night of passion brought a year's worth of remorse, like last time. What if her daughter walked in on them?

Just then, a little voice from the hallway said, "Mommy."

The heat of the moment cooled, as if someone had surprised them with the Ice Bucket Challenge.

"I'm coming, Lottie," Heather sang out.

As she jumped off the couch, Zack snagged her hand. "This isn't over, darlin'. Only postponed."

And needed to stay that way. Heather didn't want her child catching them in a compromising position. Better to focus their energies on catching her in-laws, instead.

CHAPTER THIRTEEN

Both Heather and Lottie spent a restless night in their host's bed.

Not the bed's fault, by any means.

For Heather's part, she dreamed of slipping out to join Zack on the couch, where he proved himself a magician extraordinaire. She woke—her throat dry, her body thirsting for him.

Lottie's dreams took a darker tone.

When they talked about them, Heather gathered they had less to do with the usual monster and more with pre-show jitters. To take Lottie's mind off her nerves, Heather made a promise. Lottie could, at last, get her ears pierced.

She'd been begging since age four. Now at six—practically seven—Heather figured the request was more than a passing fancy.

After breakfast, they unpacked their suitcase. Lottie wanted to wear her favorite dress—a Christmasy green velour. Heather suggested she pair it with cute snowflake leggings to keep her legs cozy warm. Heather fell back on her tan pantsuit, but wore it with a red top, to add her own Christmas flair.

They dropped into Romancing the Stone and Zack's mom showed them the choices for starter earrings. Lottie picked out a simple, gold-plated ball—one of the least expensive choices on display. Though, Heather caught her eyeing the stud with the garnet stone.

Her birthday gem.

"What do you think of this one, Lottie?" Heather asked, pointing to it.

"Isn't it *'spensive*, Mommy?"

Money concerns from a first grader? It broke Heather's heart.

That, and the fear she wouldn't be around to celebrate Lottie's birthday with her. If the judge found Heather guilty at her January court date, it could be years before she saw her daughter again. She wanted Lottie to have a keepsake—something precious that she could cherish forever—as Heather had cherished those hoop earrings from her own parents.

"What if we stretched out the purchase for three occasions: the show, Christmas, and for turning seven?"

Lottie nodded, resembling a Lisa Simpson bobble-head.

"Garnets are a great choice," Diane told them. "Good for added confidence. They'll get you through the performance without a hitch."

She asked Lottie to sit in a chair and applied cleaning solution to her earlobes. "Now, I need you to stay real still, sugar."

The first stud went in without a whimper. When she finished the second, Diane held up a mirror so Lottie could see.

The girl's smile out-sparkled the gems.

Diane showed Lottie how to care for her new piercings and presented her with a sucker and a Courage Certificate, which featured the Cowardly Lion wearing his Bravery Medal, and a red bow in his mane.

From that point on, Diane became Lottie's new bestie.

Zack's mom reached under the cash desk for a calculator. "Piercings are free with the purchase of earrings. With your friends and family discount that comes to…five dollars."

Heather almost dropped her purse. "Diane, that's really kind of you, but I can't…"

"Well, *I* can." She squeezed Heather's hand. "Please, let me help you with this. Zack speaks so highly of y'all, and Lottie is such a darlin'."

Diane proved her generosity, again, by sitting with Heather and Zack during the performance of *The Nutcracker*, taking on the role of Lottie's absent grandparents.

From the moment the curtain opened on the Stahlbaums' living room with its gigantic Christmas tree, the production shone with homespun charm. Even when Duncan Frost sneezed and all the other toy soldiers burst out laughing.

When Lottie made her first appearance as a snowflake, Heather's heart caught. Of the five little girls on stage, only her daughter held back. She froze, squinting at the bright lights. Then, as if some internal switch snapped on, Lottie held out her arms and skipped around the stage with the others, twinkling for all her might.

At the end, the cast took their bows. One small boy, startled by the applause, covered his ears and howled, while Lottie basked in the attention, practically glowing as she waved to Heather from the stage.

The spectators leapt up and gave the show a standing ovation. Heather hid her happy tears from Zack, who stuck two fingers in his mouth and let out a loud, appreciative whistle—as proud of Lottie as if she were his own.

The man would make some kid a great dad.

When Heather went backstage to meet her daughter, she spotted Ruth and Wenda lavishing her with hugs. As soon as they saw Heather, though, they bolted. Which suited Heather fine. She'd prefer to stay clear of her in-laws until she devised a way to expose their part in the accusations against her. In the meantime, Heather didn't want to deprive her daughter of their affection.

While Heather contemplated it all, Lottie wandered over to Duncan and his friends, who were mesmerized by Zack and his now-famous coin trick.

"Do you think maybe there's some money in *your* ear?" he asked Lottie, his voice low and gentle.

She looked at Zack warily, but didn't protest, didn't slink away when he approached. He kept his movements slow as he reached behind her head and revealed a shiny quarter.

"You can keep this one, if you want."

Lottie shot a glance Heather's way for approval. Then her little hand reached out to Zack, who dropped the coin into the girl's palm.

A great dad, indeed.

Heather ran up and kissed him, full on the lips. One of Duncan's friends—Nathan, she imagined—voiced a resounding, "Yuck!" But none of the other kids seemed to mind.

Once Zack saw his mom to her own car, he drove Heather and Lottie to his place—the latter snoozing in the backseat after the day's excitement.

"That trick with Lottie was pretty amazing," she whispered.

"We're a long way from buddies, but it's a start."

A start. Yet, their stay in Carol Falls was coming to an end. With the Winter Recital over, and their investigations stalled, there was nothing to keep Heather in town.

Except Zack. Her unreliable car. And the wedding.

The old Radcliffe Mansion was the perfect spot for a reception.

Rich and eccentric, the Radcliffes were one of the founding families of Carol Falls and had built their Italianate-style home about a block from Mayor Lincoln's current residence, with building supplies imported from Europe.

Some said the place was haunted. Some said the Radcliffes merely had a string of bad luck—especially after Charles Sr. took a nosedive off a skyscraper following the Stock Market Crash of 1929. Whatever the case, the last surviving relative had donated what remained of the estate to the town. After its restoration, the mansion reclaimed its title as a hotspot for special events, all held in the elegant main-floor ballroom, which once hosted such luminaries as Rudy Vallée and Calvin Coolidge.

Heather and Zack arrived on site early, already dressed in their black serving attire, to help with the set-up for the reception. At the front door, artists erected a beautiful arch through which the wedding party and the guests would enter. Carved entirely from ice, the impressive ten-foot sculpture displayed a heart at the apex. So as not to get in the workers' way, Heather and Zack entered through the kitchen at the rear.

She got busy preparing the tables for the celebration. Whoever the bride was, she'd picked a lovely pallet—pale gray tablecloths, silver-rimmed plates, and forest green accents—wonderful choices for a winter wedding. These hues were echoed in the floral arrangements Heather set on each table. There were even blossoms, strung together and suspended overhead, similar to beaded curtains—something she'd seen in a magazine while waiting with Lottie at her pediatrician's office. These cascading flowers displayed the forest green and silver colors, but added festive touches of snow white and cranberry.

Ian's cousin was a lucky guy to be marrying someone with such refined taste.

As Heather folded the napkins with a classic French pleat, she reflected on the past week and couldn't stop smiling. True, the court case still hung over her, and she'd yet to come up with a plan to investigate her in-laws' participation in the evidence against her, but staying with Zack had been a wonderful choice.

He'd helped her drop off résumés and even driven her to a couple of interviews. Better yet, the three of them ate together, went skating at the park's rink and, one evening, when she'd decided to give herself a pedicure, Zack swept in to add the polish. She'd seen men do that in movies, but never in real life.

If that wasn't sweet enough, when Lottie said she needed a pedicure too, Zack learned how to paint polka dots on little toes. That Lottie trusted him enough to allow him to do it, warmed Heather all over.

And those goodnight kisses of his made Heather sizzle.

She looked over at him as he readied the bar, his dreamy eyes fixed on her. Was he thinking the same thing? With Lottie at Diane's house for the night, she and Zack might be able to explore more than each other's cuticles.

A dangerous path, indeed.

Until the charges against her were dropped, she couldn't allow things to go further between them. It wouldn't be fair to Zack.

Heather continued with her work, teaching a couple other employees what to do with all the cutlery. Passing the mountain of presents on the gift table reminded her of a second mystery package she'd found on Zack's doorstep. This one contained crayons and a coloring book. She would have suspected it came from Ruth and Wenda, if the first package hadn't appeared on their own front porch. Whoever sent it must have realized the change in her own locale. Not hard to do in a small town, but a little creepy.

Was someone following her?

A big arm wrapped around her waist, jolting her. Zack's cologne filled her senses. "Got word that the church service is finished. The guests should be arriving in the next fifteen to twenty minutes."

"We'll be ready," she promised.

She finished pouring the ice water just as the first invitees trickled through the wedding arch. Many stood talking, some ordering drinks from Zack.

Heather was startled to see her lawyer in the group, with Robin

Redmond on his arm. Taking in Spencer's tux and the pretty dress Robin wore, Heather knew they weren't there to see her. They had to be friends of the bride and groom.

They conversed with the fire chief, Ian King, before being joined by an older couple—a petite, well-dressed woman and a tall, still-handsome man whose thinness hinted at a recent illness. Since Spence displayed a comfortable familiarity around the pair, and noticing a few similar features, Heather assumed they were his parents.

Hot on their trail, she spied one of the kids from Lottie's play—Nathan Boychuk—along with his dad, Peter, and his mom, Linda, who was carrying a toddler. The accountant shared a kiss with his wife, and then moseyed over to get refreshments for his family.

When Sylvia and Harold Frost arrived and began greeting the early guests, Heather started to wonder whose wedding reception she'd blundered into.

Then the police made their entrance.

Josephine Frost, swathed in forest green like the other bridesmaids, strode into the ballroom on the arm of Noel Fletcher. More alarming, the officers' presence heralded the appearance of someone she'd tried her best to avoid, until now.

She spotted young Marcus first, carrying his ever-present electronic notebook. On his heels his mother, April, emerged from the arch with Marcus' new dad, Jim Frost.

In the past, she would have run. Get out of there as fast as she could.

No more.

The party was short-staffed. If Heather left now, she might jeopardize the bride's perfect day. Not to mention, she needed the paycheck. She kept her head down and vowed to work as hard as she could to make the festivities a success.

The rest of the bridal party arrived and began a receiving line for their guests. Garret Frost looked dashing in a gray tux and his bride, Lily Parker, glittered in a similarly colored, beaded gown—her blond hair piled high and held with an emerald clip.

All eyes were on the couple.

Perfect.

Quickly, Heather assigned two other waitresses to replace her at the head table, which would avoid any awkwardness between her and Jim. That morning, she'd shown the women the proper way to serve from the right, clear from the left, and how to carry several plates at a time. Both expertly presented the appetizers, salad and main course—chicken with a maple, apple and cranberry stuffing. Meanwhile, Heather tended to a larger section at the back of the room.

Clinking glasses, Garret and Lily stood and kissed. Heather couldn't help but remember her own wedding day. However, when she pictured her groom, she didn't visualize Chase. Not anymore. In her mind, he'd been replaced by a certain volunteer firefighter with chocolate brown eyes.

Garret gave a toast to his best man and brother, Jim. Lily did the same for her sister, the matron of honor, who'd come all the way from Colorado with their parents, her husband and three children.

"I'd also like to propose a toast to my…" Garret clasped Lily to his side. "…to *our* son and ring bearer, Duncan."

"Good thing me and SpongeBob got to practise at Uncle Jim's wedding," Duncan replied, his excited voice filling the huge space without a microphone. "We didn't drop the ring this time."

Chuckles went through the crowd. Heather had to laugh too, though she wasn't sure about this SpongeBob character. Sure, the name came from an animated program, but Lord only knew what Duncan meant. When the guests fell silent again, the boy continued.

"And you know what? I'd like to *suppose* a toast, myself." He lifted his glass of apple juice. "To my new mommy. Thanks for making my daddy smile again."

Garret wiped his eyes and topped Duncan's speech by sharing another kiss with his bride. But, apparently, Duncan wasn't ready to give up the spotlight.

"I also want to thank Lily," the boy went on. "For being patient with SpongeBob when he has an accident on the floor."

Heather now understood that Duncan had named his puppy SpongeBob, and laughed even harder.

Before the kid could cut loose with his stand-up routine, a familiar voice rose over the speakers. "It's time to open the dance floor," Jim Frost announced from the small stage. "The DJ has all your favorites ready to go, but I'm starting the night off with a little song I wrote for the happy couple."

Jim sang, accompanying himself on the guitar. The words spoke of longing for someone, and having that longing fulfilled. Themes Heather imagined Jim knew well from the way he gazed at his own bride, April.

As he sang, Garret ushered Lily to the open space in the middle of the room. They looked so heavenly dancing together, as if floating on a cloud.

Heather wished she could be so carefree, so happy.

After the applause, the lights dimmed and the DJ took over. During the next tune, Lily's father cut in and danced with his daughter, while Garret took his mom for a spin. Then it was Harold's turn to dance with Lily, so Garret wound up with her mother. Soon the bridal party paired up with their usual partners, though Ian sat on the sidelines, alone in the shadows with his drink.

At the DJ's invitation, most of the guests joined in…while Heather cleared the last of the plates, feeling a little like Cinderella after the ball.

The guests kept Zack hopping.

Though some wanted a beer or Baileys, most enjoyed the non-alcoholic winter drinks of warm apple cider, eggnog and hot chocolate—a big hit among the kids. Especially topped with the candy canes and marshmallows Zack had on hand. Ideas he'd borrowed from Kate's Kitchen.

Now, with the guests either dancing or dispersing, he had time to enjoy the music. And the view of a certain blond server who, in his opinion, outshone the bride.

The woman who, if she'd stayed in town last Christmas, would be his now.

While he looked for her through the swaying bodies, he noticed the ever-graceful Sylvia Frost walking toward him, most likely to let him know the timing for last call.

As he came around the bar to meet her, she faltered. Zack caught her with one arm and led her to a chair. "Are you okay?"

"Yes. Fine."

She didn't look it. Not with that pale face.

"I'll get you some water." He filled a glass, keeping his eye on her the whole time. Whatever had made her feel faint, it wasn't liquor. She'd had only ginger ale all evening.

She took a sip of the water.

"Feeling better?"

"Much. Thank you."

"You're welcome. Now, you stay here. I'll go get your husband."

Before he could take a step, she latched on to his arm. "Please don't bother him. Or the children. I don't want to ruin the celebration. And it's nothing. *Really.* It's just been a busy month—with the play and the wedding. I'm fine."

Zack disagreed, but it wasn't his place to interfere with her wishes. He stayed and talked with her for a few minutes, mostly about when he should close the bar.

He laid a hand on her shoulder. "You sure you're all right?"

"Perfectly. Thanks again." Sylvia handed her empty glass to him, stood, and made her way back to the head table for the cake cutting.

At eight o'clock, the happy couple, and their little boy, bid everyone goodnight.

Proud that she'd managed to get through the evening without ruffling any feathers, Heather gathered the last of the stray glasses and placed them in a plastic bin to carry to the kitchen.

"May I have this dance?" Zack stood beside her, his hand outstretched, waiting to take hers.

She set the bin on the nearest table. "Are we allowed?"

"Why not? Most everyone's gone." He spun her on to the parquet floor with a surprisingly slick move.

"You have secret talents, sir."

"You have secrets, too. Want to tell me why you were avoiding the Frosts all evening?"

She grimaced. "I thought I was being so covert."

"You were. Everyone else was looking at the bride and groom. Me? I was looking at you."

"Hope you didn't spill much."

"Not a chance. I'm a trained professional."

Zack twirled her again, but she tripped over herself, her legs stiff and awkward.

"At first, I figured you were upset because of the cops," he told her. "I hadn't thought about them being here when I suggested you for the job. Sorry about that."

"Watching Josephine Frost intercept the bouquet with that wide receiver move was worth it."

They danced long enough for Heather to revel in the closeness of him, to believe he'd forgotten about his earlier question. When he kissed her, she forgot all about it, too.

"Having you in my arms feels so right, Heather. There's nothing stopping us now. We could have our own wedding dance. At our own wedding." He lowered himself onto one knee. "What do you say?"

This was the moment she'd longed for. The moment she'd feared.

"Wait, Zack."

She couldn't let him propose. Not while she still faced imprisonment. And not with this secret between them. Time would relieve the first hurdle. The second, was hers alone to resolve.

"I haven't answered your question about why I avoided the Frosts tonight."

He stood. His gaze, both hesitant and curious, paralyzed her tongue.

She could lie. That would be easy. Or, she could tell the truth and sacrifice her future with him. But if she couldn't be honest—if Heather couldn't reveal who she was, faults included—what was she offering him? Only a plastic version of herself.

"I wasn't trying to avoid all the Frosts. Only Jim."

"You two have a history?"

She should have expected the hint of jealousy in his tone. "We do. But not the way you're thinking." Heather wrapped her arms around her middle, cocooning herself from the bad memories. "Last Christmas, I did something very foolish. Very hurtful."

"You're not the hurtful type."

"I hate to shatter your impression of me, but I can't let you propose without telling you the truth."

Heather prayed he'd understand. Prayed he'd, at least, forgive her. She laced her hands together and spoke quickly, wanting the confession over and done.

"I tried to come between April and Jim."

Zack gave her a blank stare. "What? Why?"

A touch of vertigo hit her, so she widened her stance for balance. It was as if she were on the edge of a precipice. Once she answered him, there'd be no going back. She'd have to accept his reaction, whatever it may be.

She faced him, and her shame, head-on. "Because I wanted Jim to marry *me*."

Zack clamped his teeth together. His jaw burned as if she'd slapped him. "You were playing both of us?"

"No. I didn't mean to. I was desperate, Zack. I needed to present a stable family to child services so I could get Lottie back."

"And I wasn't good enough for you?" He raised a hand to rub his forehead and saw her flinch. Did she really think he'd hit her?

With her history, Zack guessed she did. He stepped back to give her space, softening his tone when he spoke again. "*I* would have married you."

Her eyes darkened. "I've no doubt you would have rescued me. It's typically you."

What was that supposed to mean? And why was she suddenly mad at *him?*

"I realize now, I had to rescue myself," she explained, her words coming out in short bursts. "Maybe a part of me knew that even a year ago. That's why I left town. I'd caused enough pain. I wanted to protect you from that."

Since when did *he* need protecting? "What the hell are you talking about?"

"I barely knew Jim, but there I was, trying to use him and his family's good name. I would have used anything and anyone to hold my child again."

She reached out as if to touch him, then apparently thought better of it. "I didn't want to use *you*, Zack."

He didn't know what to say, what to think. He saw the same Heather—same blue eyes, same blond hair, same lovely face. The woman he'd wanted all week. All *year*.

Identical on the outside, but different on the inside. Changed. So unlike the person he'd known. Or thought he knew.

"Sorry to interrupt," a male voice said.

Zack turned to find Jim Frost—the last man he wanted to see right now. Sure, the guy could play guitar like a pro, but his timing was way off.

"Garret left me in charge of the finances."

"What's this?" Zack snatched the envelope Jim offered and ripped it open.

"Your pay. Thanks for helping us out tonight."

Heather's arms hung at her sides. "I didn't realize this was your brother's wedding when I agreed to serve tables. If I'd known, I never would have—"

"Not a problem," Jim said, and extended her payment again. "We appreciate all you did tonight."

"I'm sorry about the trouble I caused you last Christmas."

"You apologized then."

Jim's gaze shifted. Zack looked in the same direction and saw April and Marcus, coats on and heads bent over the boy's electronic notebook—enjoying each other's company while they waited.

"I gotta admit," Jim said, focusing on Heather again. "It took awhile to forgive you for messing with my life. But I have." He folded her hand around the envelope. "You should, too."

He gave her a brief smile and rejoined his beautiful family.

Zack couldn't look at Heather, couldn't figure out what to make of the exchange he'd just heard. He'd been about to propose, for God's sake. To make a fool of himself. Over a woman who'd dumped him as soon as something better came along.

Some might say he'd made a lucky escape.

Because if it had taken Jim Frost awhile to forgive Heather, Zack figured he'd have to survive a couple of lifetimes to do the same.

They drove to Zack's place, Heather holding the cold cheque in her hand. No tunes played on the radio, this time—only dead air.

She'd made up her mind. It was time to pack her bags and leave. Before Zack threw her out.

With her car still up on blocks in his driveway, she wasn't sure where she'd end up. Without a steady job, she wouldn't last long in Burlington. Nor could she go to her sister's in New York, not with the judge's order for her to remain in Vermont. She might eventually have to bite the bullet and crawl back to her parents' house in Montpelier.

If they'd take her.

For now, she'd go to the local hotel. She never used her credit card, except in emergencies, and this classified as one—the way Zack white-knuckled the steering wheel, his handsome face tight, his jaw set.

As of tonight, she'd officially outstayed her welcome.

She should have told him the rest of the story. That, once they'd made love, she couldn't marry Jim, even if he'd wanted her. Not after Zack had shown her what true love meant.

Just as well she hadn't found the words to express her feelings. In the heat of the moment, she doubted he would have believed her anyway.

When they pulled up to his bungalow, Heather caught a glimpse of a person crouching on the porch. And, in the dimness of the streetlight, she could see the outline of another square package.

She jumped out of Zack's truck, before it came to a stop. With railings on the sides of the porch, the stranger had to either vault over the barriers, or come down the main steps. Heather intercepted the person at the bottom of the stairs.

She grabbed a thin arm, realized she was holding a female. "Who are you?"

The smaller woman wrenched away and collided with Zack, who'd parked the truck and come to join the action. With the odds against her, the woman gave up the fight. She pulled back her hoodie.

"Merry?"

Heather recognized the purple-haired woman from the bookstore. Zack obviously knew her by name.

"I really appreciate the gifts. Lottie does, too."

"You're welcome." Merry's gaze darted between them. "I should be getting home now."

Zack stepped in front of her. "I hear you live near Billy Boy's so my place is really out of your way. What brings you here?"

"I-I-I wanted to drop something nice off for the little girl. I'd heard about Heather's troubles and with it being close to Christmas…"

"Interesting that you're feeling so generous," he said, his voice hard. "Especially to someone you identified as an arsonist."

Merry made a run for it, but Zack blocked her with his body a second time. "I'm going to ask you again. Why are you here?"

The woman's face crumpled, tears in her eyes. Immediately, Zack backed off.

Not Heather. "Answer him. Why are you here?"

"I felt bad," Merry blubbered. "I wanted to do something to make up for…"

"For what?"

When Merry recoiled, Heather touched the young woman's hand. "What did you feel bad about?"

"For lying," Merry whispered between sobs. "About seeing you at Billy Boy's that night."

Heather knew all about lies. Knew that, sometimes, you did bad things to help the people you love.

Zack had his cell phone out and punched in three digits. Calling the police, no doubt. They'd be on their way, soon. But Heather couldn't resist one more question.

"Why, Merry? Why did you lie about me? Were you protecting someone?"

Merry nodded and accepted the tissue Heather offered. "Yes. My boyfriend."

CHAPTER FOURTEEN

Two anxious days later, Heather found herself gazing at the hollowed-out ruin of Billy Boy's.

The walls remained upright and solid, though some were blackened now. Others showed scabs where the paint had bubbled up from the heat of the fire. Still, her old workplace looked familiar.

Familiar, yet damaged. Much the same as her relationship with Zack.

The chilled air formed an icy wall between them as he paced the length of the bar, keyed-up about their looming task. Or was it her presence that had him so uptight?

Perhaps she'd find a moment to ask him once this was over. For now, Heather focused on staying warm. She slid her hands into her coat pockets—better there than fluttering around betraying her nerves. She hated confrontations...and this one would be off the charts.

Twenty minutes after their scheduled appointment, and just as Heather was about to give up, Billy Boychuk walked into the bar, his brother Peter in tow. The two men may have planned to take the upper hand with their late arrival. But Heather held all the dice now.

At least, she hoped so.

"Thanks for coming, gentlemen. I have a business proposition for you."

The brothers shared an uneasy glance.

"You wanna buy this place from me? Fix it up?"

"Hardly," Heather answered Billy, trying her best to sound self-assured. "I'm offering to fix *you* up. With a willing patsy."

She gestured for their surprise guest to come out from the kitchen. Billy had little reaction to Merry's entrance, but his brother's mouth sprung open.

"I told them, Peter," the purple-haired woman announced. "I told them everything."

Billy grabbed his brother by the lapels of his snappy wool coat and shook. "You talked to her about our plan?"

Peter slammed his fists into Billy's chest and pushed him away. "Shut up."

"Chill out, both of you." Zack pulled the brothers apart. "Time for Heather to do the talking."

She swallowed her fears, knowing everything depended on her now. Heather needed to play her part to the hilt for their scheme to work.

"It's a simple deal," she began. "Merry's told us all about your insurance scam. And, since I may end up in prison because of it, I want my fair share of the take."

The brothers cried in outrage. Zack grabbed them by their collars and hoisted them onto their toes. "Keep it up," Zack growled, "and I'll have you dancin' like ballerinas."

The two fell silent and stopped struggling. Zack rewarded their compliance by releasing his hold, but he stood guard, ready to intervene again, if necessary.

Thank God he provided a good, strong front. Not Heather. Each heartbeat sent a tremor through her body. She only hoped her adversaries were too intimidated by Zack's muscle to notice.

"As far as splitting the money, there's the two of you." The Boychuks didn't contradict her, so she went on "Merry wants a cut now. And you've got the Trivetts—"

"Not them," Peter interjected.

Heather didn't bother to contain her surprise. It fit in perfectly with the character she portrayed. "You didn't pay the Trivetts to lie about me?"

Billy approached her, his hands outstretched. Her old boss looked surprisingly contrite, given the circumstances. "Sorry, Heather. I don't know how they came up with that story about you. Honest."

Another puzzle. One she'd have to solve later. "Fine, then. No Trivetts. Even better. That leaves us with a five-way split."

Peter hitched a thumb at Zack. "He gets a cut, too? How come?"

"I'm outta job because of you," Zack snapped. "That's how come."

Billy fanned the air with his hands, trying to quell the situation. "Okay, okay. We'll split the insurance money five ways. But not equally. It's my bar, after all. I'm the one taking the risk."

"Not the way I see it." Heather braced herself for the final assault. "I want my money off the top. And I want half."

"Half?" Peter scoffed. "Why should we give you half?"

"Because otherwise, I'll go to the police with my new friend, Merry." Heather almost wished she smoked. If she were in a film noir, this would be the perfect time to light up. "If you want me to take the fall, you'll have to make it worth my while."

"But *half*, Heather? Give me a break, will ya?" Billy lowered his chin and looked up at her, like a sad Basset Hound. "I'm sorry about your arrest. I really am. I knew it wasn't you, but I couldn't say anything. Couldn't defend you without implicating myself."

"Because you set the fire?"

"Yeah...but it was Peter's idea."

"Will you shut your mouth?"

Billy ignored his brother. "He knew I had financial problems. Enough gambling debt to strangle myself. Pete suggested the fire and the insurance money as the way out. But I'm the one who rigged the lamp."

Heather pretended to consider Billy's predicament. "Okay...what are you willing to pay me to keep my mouth shut and go to jail for you? Make me an offer."

"I'll give you ten grand."

She snorted. "Make me a real offer, Billy."

"Twenty then. Twenty's more than generous."

"I was thinking...a hundred thousand."

"Are you crazy, woman? By the time I split the rest four ways, I'll have next to nothing."

"What about the cash in the safe?" Zack asked. "Where'd that end up?"

"Huh? What cash?"

Zack stared Billy down, advancing on him—a hunter stalking his prey. "Don't act innocent with me. I was here when we opened the safe, remember?"

Billy's gaze shot around the room. Perhaps searching for a plausible way to explain the missing money. Heather doubted he'd find the answer written in soot.

"It's gone, man," he said, his vocal range spiking upward. "I needed it to make good on my immediate debts."

"You were an idiot to take it," Peter said, taunting his brother.

"So you keep telling me. Claimed it would trip us up." Billy's lip curled. "But your bit of lovin' on the side did that."

As the two Boychuks locked fists, the police stepped out of their hiding places. Noel Fletcher cuffed Billy, while Josephine Frost read the man his Miranda rights.

Peter made use of his runner's training and sprinted to the door. There, he collided with Officer Wedge, who entered with another set of handcuffs.

The accountant backed away. "Whoa. I didn't set the fire."

"Helping your brother with a fraudulent insurance claim is still a crime," Wedge told him.

"I didn't know about the fraud. I never suggested anything to him."

"That's not what we heard," Joey piped in as Heather removed the police wire she'd been wearing. "You've got a lot of explaining in store, Peter. Especially to your wife and children."

Peter's mouth tightened as Wedge locked him in cuffs. The only sound left in the room was the officer's voice as he told the man his rights.

And Merry's sobs.

"I'm sorry for my part in this," she said to Heather. "Peter seemed so worldly, so sophisticated. When he took an interest in me...when he said he loved me..."

Heather offered the young woman another tissue. She'd already heard how Merry met Peter when he'd come into the bookstore to run with the owner, Mark Lauder—the man who wrote Lottie's play.

"Peter said he agreed to have a second child with his wife, hoping it would save their marriage. But it didn't work. He said they slept in separate rooms and that he continued to live with her only because his divorce lawyer told him to—so he could get a better share of the property and ensure his chances of joint custody." Merry's chin quivered. "I realize now he had no intention of leaving Linda. I was stupid to fall for his lies."

Heather sympathized with the young woman. She hoped that by helping them today, the police would go easy on Merry for making false accusations.

As the male officers led the two cuffed men out of the building, Heather approached Joey and handed her the surveillance device.

"Thanks for agreeing to wear this. It took us awhile to convince Chief Slayton to invest in it."

"I was happy to help." And prove her own innocence.

"You played your part well. Didn't sound the least bit nervous."

Heather knew that skill had evolved during her years with Chase—all those times she'd received a beating, then picked herself off the floor and went to work, acting as if nothing happened.

"We may have to hire you for other undercover operations," Joey added with a joking lilt.

Heather had no interest in that. She was through living a lie.

"Of course, the charges against you will be dropped," Joey promised.

"Thanks. But I still don't understand about the Trivetts. They said they saw a blond woman at the bar the night of the fire and they identified me."

"A lie. Connor now claims a stranger—a beefy male—spoon-fed him that story. Promised Connor enough money to see him through college and then some, if he'd implicate you. The stranger gave Connor ten thousand as a retainer, then came back and threatened him physically, swearing to mess him up royally if he didn't go through with his accusations. We're pretty confident the beefy male was Billy."

"He just denied it on tape. Said he didn't know why the Trivetts involved me."

"Probably to save face. You were Billy's employee, after all. He knew you personally and victimized you anyway. And Connor, no doubt, fabricated the threats to his person hoping to reduce his culpability and gain sympathy. At least in his own eyes."

"What about Mrs. Trivett?"

"Connor gave her extra pain meds after her operation, making her more susceptible to his suggestions. We believe she's innocent in all this."

"But Connor knew Billy, didn't he?" Heather understood the college student had been staying with his grandmother in Billy's upstairs suite. "Why would he blame a stranger for the bribe?"

"We suspect the kid will sing a different tune, now that Billy's confessed."

"And my earring? How did Connor get it?"

"You're not a hundred percent sure when you lost it, right? Maybe it happened while you were working here for Billy. Maybe he had it all this time." Joey frowned, perplexed over that part of the case too, Heather guessed. "I'll look into it, but I know the chief is ready to close this case."

The policewoman shook her head. "I'm glad I won't be there when Linda Boychuk finds out about her husband. But I will have to tell my parents. Peter's been the accountant at the farm for years. They'll have to go back through the records. If he was behind the insurance fraud, there may be other irregularities."

Joey gave Heather a tired smile, put her arm around Merry and guided the young woman out of the building. That left Heather and Zack alone. In spite of their success, a cold wall still separated them.

"I guess I should be going."

"Back to Burlington?"

She nodded. "Thanks for fixing my car."

It wasn't the most reliable vehicle, but she needed it to continue her sessions with Juliette. Not only was the woman a skilled psychologist, she'd proven to be an excellent business manager.

She'd already found two other bookkeeping clients for Heather. And had put in a good word for her with the operator of the local women's shelter. Balancing their books was strictly a volunteer position, but one Heather relished. Not only would it give her an extra credit on her résumé, more importantly, it would provide Heather with a way to give back to the community, and empower her at the same time. A career she'd thought she'd buried was now resurrected. Along with the rest of her life.

She only wished that life included Zack.

"We should talk about this. About what I did last Christmas—"

"You already explained. But too late to do any good. You should have told me the truth then."

And the truth was important to him. She knew that.

"What can I say to—"

"Nothing, Heather. If we can't be open and honest with each other...if I can't trust you...what's the point?"

"I know I hurt you, Zack, and I didn't mean to—"

He jammed his hands in his pockets and gazed at that staff photo on the wall, tuning her out. She'd met him while working in the bar. Now, they were ending their relationship in the burnt-out mess where it began.

With Zack's need to rescue, Heather didn't know if she could become the strong woman she wanted to be—needed to be—for herself and her daughter.

But, he was right. She owed him the truth. Especially, about how she felt.

"I have no interest in any other man. Not since that night we spent together. I fell in love with you then. And I've loved you ever since."

She took a step closer, wanting to end things on a positive note with a kiss, but his face was a hard mask.

"I'll stop by your mother's place and pick up Lottie."

Then she'd go to Ruth's and give her and Wenda the whole-hearted apology they deserved. She felt terrible for suspecting them, given the circumstantial evidence—the same kind of evidence that had led to Heather's own arrest. However eccentric, her in-laws loved Lottie, and Lottie loved them. Heather didn't want to be the one to keep them apart.

Afterward, she'd call her sister and let Fern know the charges were dropped, that her portion of the bail money would be returned. Along with Zack's.

"We'll head back to your house, collect our stuff, and get out of your hair."

He said nothing, just slid his gaze to the floor.

Saddened she could do no more, Heather hoisted her purse higher on her shoulder, the lucky moonstone dangling by her hand.

Not so lucky after all.

No matter what, she'd always be grateful to Zack, for helping her prove her innocence and for giving her the greatest gift—freedom—and being reunited with her daughter for Christmas.

Heather took a final look at him, recording his image in her mind like a snapshot. Then she wrapped her coat tight against her and walked out into the winter's sun.

Alone, Zack wandered the bar.

What would happen to the place now? Would someone buy it? Do the repairs? With Heather's bail money back in his bank, he could consider that kind of investment.

Heather.

He shoved a piece of debris aside with the toe of his boot, feeling equally discarded.

No. That wasn't the right word.

Betrayed. That was closer. Betrayed by both Heather and Billy.

He climbed in his truck and drove past his mother's house. No sign of life there. Heather must have picked up Lottie already, which left his mom free to enjoy some gift shopping.

By now Heather would be at his place, packing her things. Zack didn't want to run into her, so he checked out the action on the Main Square.

With only two days until Christmas, folks were bustling in and out of the stores, arms laden with parcels. Every business, every lamppost, glittered with colored ornaments and leafy boughs.

"Bah, humbug."

His cell phone rang. Zack pulled over to answer and was surprised to hear Mrs. Frost's voice on the other end, saying, "Hello," and identifying herself.

"I'm wondering if you wouldn't mind stopping by the farm, Zack."

He certainly had some time to kill. He could check on Sylvia and make sure she was okay after her fall. Following that, he'd pop around to see Ian. Maybe grab a beer with the boss. Ask about his Christmas plans.

"When?"

"Are you free at the moment?"

"Sure. I'm on my way."

Zack left the town's center and swung past the old Radcliffe Mansion. A mental image sprang up—of himself, on his knees at Heather's feet, and about to propose.

He stomped on the gas pedal and took the next hill at rollercoaster speed. Seeing Frost Farms spread out before him brought Sylvia's call back to mind.

How'd she get his cell number? From Ian?

Guess he'd find out soon enough.

Zack followed the lane to the two-story clapboard home, veiled in snow and surrounded by evergreens. Red, blue and green Christmas lights—sparkling even at this time of day—created a dotted outline of the porch.

The festive surroundings depressed Zack more. He'd never bothered to decorate his own home. Without a family, he'd never seen any reason. Now, he pictured a Christmas tree in the corner of his living room, and a certain little blond-haired girl sitting beside it, opening presents with her mother.

Only that wasn't going to happen this year. Or ever.

Zack parked and approached the house, admiring the large wreath on the front door as he climbed the stairs to the porch. When he knocked, the door swung open to reveal Duncan Frost, wearing snow pants.

"You the doorman these days?"

"Nope," the boy answered in all seriousness. "I'm going to visit Ian.

The fire chief had an apartment over the free-standing garage. Bundling up was a good move on Duncan's part.

"While my parents are on their honeymoon, Ian's looking after SpongeBob and Scout—that's Lily's dog. Grandma's allergic, so they can't stay here."

"Bummer," Zack replied, guessing at appropriate six-year-old lingo. Duncan gave him a half-hearted fist bump. "Is your grandmother around?"

"She's in the kitchen." He pointed toward the back of the house. "Better take your boots off before you come in, though, or you know what? You won't get any cookies."

Zack muffled a laugh behind his collar. As the boy disappeared through the front door in search of puppy love, Zack started his sock-footed trek down the wood-paneled hall. On his way, he heard Mrs. Frost's voice and smelled the aroma of her famous maple cookies. He followed both to the kitchen.

Within the cozy butter-colored walls, he spotted Sylvia—two coffee cups in front of her on the large oak table. He hadn't noticed another car outside, so he hadn't expected her to have another visitor. Or for that guest to be his own mother.

"Hi," he said, feeling like he'd just walked into a setup.

"Zack, thanks for coming. Would you like some coffee?"

Sylvia used the arms of the chair to lift herself. Sure, the woman was getting on in years, but she'd always been energetic. Had the tumble at the reception affected her more than she wanted to admit?

He gestured for her to sit again. "I'm glad you called. How're you doing?" He hoped Sylvia would read his unspoken message. Understand his concern.

"I'm fine, thanks."

He doubted that. Whatever the two women had been discussing, the gravity of it still hung in the air. He wished he'd gone with Duncan to play with the dogs, instead.

Then, on top of it all, his mom gave him the evil eye. "One of the things we were talking about concerns you. And Heather."

"I'm so glad to hear the charges against her will be dropped," said the Frost matriarch.

"Me, too. But, when she picked up Lottie, I have to say, she looked pretty devastated for a free woman. I can't believe you ended things with her so harshly, Zack."

He didn't want to get into this. Especially not in the Frosts' kitchen. And definitely not in front of Sylvia. "We can discuss this later, Mom."

"No, now. You can't fault her for trying to protect her child, Zack. We may not agree with her methods, but until you've faced that situation, you can't imagine what you'd do." His mom's lips trembled as she spoke.

Zack's shoulder collided with the doorjamb. He'd taken a step back without realizing it.

"When I look at her," his mom continued, "I see myself all those years ago."

She faltered again and Sylvia grasped her hand. "You can do this, Diane. It's time to tell him the full story."

Zack's gaze ping-ponged between them. He knew his mom and Mrs. Frost were friends, but what could Sylvia possibly know that he didn't? His mom rarely spoke of her past—about her marriage to his father. In deference to her feelings, he never mentioned it either.

"Things with me and your dad started off okay. He got work on a fishing boat in Alaska, so I went with him. He'd always been a tough guy—even back in Texas. At first, I was drawn to that. He could hold his own, chopping down anyone who messed with us. So I felt safe in his company…until he turned his fists on me."

All news to Zack. He had little knowledge of his parents' early days. Wasn't sure when his father became violent. Sylvia's expression, however, remained placid, as if she'd heard it all before.

"After the first time, he said he'd never hurt me again. But that didn't last."

Same story as Heather. Zack wondered if most abused women went through a similar cycle. Reluctantly, he took the seat Sylvia offered and sat at the table with them.

"Things got worse after you were born."

The confession knocked the air from his lungs. His existence made her life worse?

"Maybe I should leave you two alone," Sylvia interjected.

"Please stay. After all, this is your kitchen." Trust his mom to make a wisecrack to put everyone at ease. "Honestly, I need you here with me, Sylvia. I'm afraid I'll chicken out, if I have to do this by myself."

She took a big breath and Zack settled in for a long story.

"I reckon your dad was envious because you got most of my attention. I'd spend the day playing with you, cuddling you. But, once your father came home, I'd do my best to focus on him. I'd hoped that would make him happy." She wiped her eyes with her napkin. "It didn't work. He used you as a way to keep me in line. He threatened to hurt you, if I ever left him."

Zack glanced at his hands—both clenched. The tension spread to his gut. "I'm sorry, Mom."

She gripped his forearm. "Don't blame yourself. Not ever. You were my one joy…the only thing that got me through those dark days."

The words sounded familiar. Hadn't Heather said the same thing to him? Zack blinked, embarrassed by the sudden moisture in his eyes. He'd always hated to see his mom cry. "Thank God, he died and freed us both."

The women exchanged glances.

"Go on, Diane. You won't get a better chance."

"A better chance for what?"

His mom frowned, stress lines appearing on her forehead. "As far as I know," she began, "your father is still alive."

Zack felt as if all the blood drained from his body. He'd broken up his share of bar fights. Gone into burning buildings without flinching. This was different. This was a shift in the world. *His* world.

Sylvia rose from her seat. "Let me get you some water."

"I don't want water. I want the truth, damn it." He slammed his palm on the table.

The women jerked to attention, deep concern in their eyes...if not fear.

Oh, geez. Here they'd been talking about his father's temper and Zack was behaving like him. "Sorry, ladies."

"You're forgiven." Sylvia rested a hand on his shoulder. "We understand this is difficult for you." Then, as if to help ease the friction, she served them each a couple of cookies from her latest batch. Zack barely tasted his.

"Please, go on, Mom."

"When your dad hurt you, I knew I had to get out. I'd been putting aside a bit of money each week, in case of emergency. We left in the middle of the night and traveled as far from Alaska as the bus and the rest of the money could took us. That was here to Carol Falls. Where I met Sylvia."

The women shared a smile. His mom's conveyed the relief she must have experienced at regaining her freedom. And discovering a new friend.

"Sylvia helped me find a place to live and get a job."

That's not all. Zack remembered the Christmas basket the Frosts sent over when he was a boy. Sylvia had always watched out for them.

She placed another sheet of cookies in the oven and returned to her chair. "When you came to live here, Zack, your youthful malleability provided us with a practical solution to prevent your father from finding you."

"What solution?"

Sylvia removed her apron before answering. "I helped your mother set up a new identity, with a different last name."

Mrs. Frost knew where to get fake ID? "I think I'll take that water, after all." He stood, needing to get rid of some of his pent-up energy.

"Glasses are in the cupboard left of the sink."

He followed the direction, and filled a glass from the tap. "Jones isn't our real name?"

"Sorry, Zack," Sylvia said. "If we'd had time, I would have come up with something far more inventive."

"It worked great," his mom assured her friend. "Being so common, it made it easier for us to hide."

Zack downed the water, wishing it were something stronger. "What about Eddie? I mean, Mr. Northrup. Does he know?"

"Oh, Zack. I'm so lucky to have found such a great guy," she said, gushing. "Eddie and I were going to tell you at Christmas dinner, but maybe it's best I prepare you now. Eddie proposed."

Zack didn't want to burst her balloon, but his mother seemed oblivious to the obvious problem. He sat beside her again. "Mom...if my father is still alive, you're still—"

"Married. I know. Eddie said he didn't care. This is his shot at a second happiness and he's taking it. He doesn't want me to get in trouble for breaking the law, though, so we're going on a cruise and, when we return, we'll tell everyone the ship's captain married us. Really, we'll be living in sin."

Zack sucked in a deep breath. His sweet mom, shacking up with a guy? Suddenly Heather's schemes paled in the face of his mother's. But he couldn't fault the woman in front of him. Not when she'd lived most of her life protecting him.

"How are you feeling about all this, Zack?" Sylvia asked.

He didn't know how to answer. *Surprised? Thankful? Lost?* "I feel like...I'm not sure who I am. What's my real last name?"

"Tanskerly," his mom told him.

He expected it to sound familiar. It didn't.

She smoothed his cheek. "I should have told you before this, but I didn't know how to begin. The more I delayed, the harder it became. And, truthfully, Zack, I was afraid you'd go looking for your father."

"After what you've just told me—he's the last person I want to meet. But..." He thought for a moment. "I could do a search online to find out if he's dead or alive. Who knows, I may demand Eddie make an honest woman of you yet."

"You don't hate me?"

Zack wrapped his arms around her. "I could never hate you, Mom. You took care of me. Both you and Sylvia did what you felt you had to." In desperate circumstances.

Like Heather.

He walked his mom to her car, parked in the Frosts' garage.

Zack started the engine, cranked the heater up high, and then backed it out for her. Just because she was a brave, capable woman didn't mean he couldn't help her out from time to time.

"What exactly happened between you and Heather?" she asked, once he joined her outside again. "Can you tell me?"

He gave her the truncated version.

"Let me get this right. You're upset because you weren't her first pick for a marriage of convenience?"

Yeah. Although, put that way, it didn't sound so appealing.

"I don't think your hurt has anything to do with jealousy. I think it's because she didn't let you come to her rescue."

He started to deny it, then remembered Heather saying something similar.

"It's good to know I raised a gentleman. A *gentle* man. But you can't go around saving damsels in distress all the time, sweetie."

She hugged him, then climbed into the driver's seat and opened the window. "Of course, you want to help the people you love. But rescuing a woman isn't the same as loving her. Honoring her, being there for her—now *that's* love. You're not always going to be able to make the bad stuff disappear. Things happen—people get sick, people die. You can't erase that, Zack. Sometimes, being the hero is about supporting the person you care for. Not taking over."

He tugged at the neck of his sweater, eager to feel cool air against his skin. He hadn't expected another lecture from his mom.

"I never thought about it that way before. After the hell she'd endured with Chase, I wanted to protect her."

To make the bad stuff go away. And to stop Heather's tears. Partly because he hated seeing them. Tears reminded him of his mom and those early days with his father. He'd felt so powerless then, so useless. As a kid he couldn't do anything to stop his dad's rage…or his mom's pain.

Now, he knew the truth. It had never been his job to fix his parents' broken marriage—any more than it had been his responsibility to fix Heather's life.

His mom was right. Sometimes the only way to help was to sit down and listen to the person you cared about. Let them share their pain, their tears. And be brave enough to share yours right back.

"I never risked admitting my feelings to her," he confessed.

"Don't you think it's about time, son?"

Zack feared it was too late. He doubted Heather would forgive him. But he could try.

He watched his mom drive away then jogged to his own vehicle. He let the wind clear off the snow as he sped to his house, parked his truck in his driveway, and ran into the living room.

"Heather? Are you here?" Zack called out, even though he already knew the answer.

He drifted from empty room to empty room, gripped by a sharp sense of loss. In the kitchen, he spied dishes on the drying rack—the last thing Heather did before leaving.

Zack dropped onto the couch, remembering their meals together, how the three of them had watched TV, explored the town on daytrips…had fun.

His house was lonely without them.

Not to mention, his life.

Heather couldn't sleep.

Back in her Burlington apartment, she was exhausted from the emotional ups and downs of the last month, but still too keyed-up to wind down.

In an attempt to return to normalcy, she'd run a load of laundry and made dinner for Lottie. They'd reviewed her homework and, after decorating their place for Christmas together, Heather tucked her tired little girl in bed.

Back in the living room, Heather put the finishing touches on their tabletop Christmas tree, which shimmered with Lottie's handmade ornaments—strings of plastic beads, Playdough stars and paper snowflakes.

Seeing the decorations made Heather smile. She felt truly blessed, truly thankful. Her love life had tanked, but she was free and with her daughter for Christmas. And every day after.

Nothing could be better.

Heather stayed busy with make-work projects. She changed into her old tracksuit, got out her iron and pressed her best job-hunting outfit. If she could find a few more bookkeeping positions, she could make ends meet. Possibly even work from home and save childcare costs, too.

She was thankful for that. Even though she missed Carol Falls. And, most especially, missed the man she'd left behind there.

A knock sounded on the door. Heather set the iron aside and looked out the peephole. Through the distorted fisheye-view, she saw dark clothing...and a man's broad back.

Zack.

Stay cool, she told her pounding heart as she flung open the door.

Out of the dimness of the hall, an object swung toward her. A stick? A cane? She put up her arm to deflect the blow.

Too late.

She heard the crack, felt a sharp explosion of pain as metal splintered bone. The tip of the weapon continued on its trajectory and struck her skull, bright spots filling her vision.

Heather fell. She heard the intruder enter...heard the door slam shut behind him...

Then everything turned black.

CHAPTER FIFTEEN

Her hearing returned first.

A rustling. A child's whimper.

Heather opened her eyes, blinked. She was on the floor, her cheek smooched against the carpet, her left arm at an awkward angle, screaming at her.

Broken. She'd had enough fractures during her marriage to know how they looked, how they felt.

She closed her eyes again and lay there as she had after one of Chase's beatings. Better to give up, to let the pain overtake her and drift into unconsciousness. Once she acknowledged he'd won, he'd leave her alone.

She heard the whimper a second time.

The light stabbed her eyes, increasing the hammering in her head and making her see double. She blinked again, gained focus and scanned the room, looking for her daughter. A sharp odor brought her to tears.

Smoke.

Heather saw the iron on the floor. During the assault, it had toppled onto the carpet, along with the clothes she'd been pressing. Now her suit was on fire.

"Mommy, Mommy…"

She had to get up, find Lottie and get out. If only her body would cooperate. When she lifted herself off the floor, the room spun, and her limbs were slow to respond to her commands.

The smoke detector blared, pummeling her head with new misery. Then she saw her attacker. The figure tugged at Lottie, dragging her across the living room and toward the front door.

It wasn't Chase. Couldn't be. With her brain fuzzy, Heather

didn't understand exactly what was going on, but one thing was clear—the stranger who'd knocked her down was trying to take Lottie.

Heather reached out with her good arm, searching for a weapon. Her hand found the object used against her—a golf club. She struggled to sit, sucking in oxygen as a wave of nausea hit her.

She shoved with her feet until her back hit against the kitchen cupboard, then dug in her heels. Her leg muscles twitched and strained as she pushed herself to a standing position. Cold rage filling her, she staggered to her daughter's side, swung her arm back and brought the club down on the assailant's head with all the might she could rally.

The blow sent shockwaves of agony through her injured arm. So much so, she dropped the weapon and fell to the floor before realizing she'd missed her target.

The club hadn't connected with the stranger's head, but a spot between his neck and shoulder. The result was pretty much the same, though. The attacker crumpled onto his back.

What the devil...

Heather stared at him—the eyes, the wide cheeks, the forehead.

Doug? Her brother-in-law? "What are you doing here?"

"You're a terrible mother—that's why I'm here. Fern deserves a child. Lottie should have been hers."

He lunged at their feet. Weaponless, Heather put all her strength into a kick, aimed where it would hurt him the most.

Doug screamed and curled into a fetal position.

With the added jolt of pain to her arm, Heather almost joined him. Sweat drenched her as blackness swooped in again. At the edge of consciousness, she heard banging at the door. Or was it the throbbing of her head?

Coughing, she forced herself past the darkness and through the smoke. She tucked her bad arm against her body, and steered Lottie toward the door.

At that moment, it burst open, and in rushed Zack with a fire extinguisher, as the flashing lights of the approaching emergency crews danced a whirling dervish over the sheer curtains.

Heather sat on the edge of the hospital bed, her left arm in a cast, held close to her body in a sling.

She fingered the bandage at her temple. The throbbing made it difficult to concentrate, or believe the offer she'd just received. She stared at the hospital phone beside her, still in shock over the last call, not to mention the events of the evening.

"Mommy!"

Her little girl ran into the room, still wearing her Hello Kitty PJs. Zack followed right behind her, carrying Lottie's winter coat. Both wore Santa hats, which Zack must have purchased at the hospital gift shop.

Heather sighed with relief. Knowing her child was okay, that Zack had kept her safe, warm and entertained, was the best medicine possible.

If only he could say the words to mend her broken heart.

"I was worried about you, Mommy."

Heather had no doubt about that. The last time she'd been in the hospital, Chase had been placed under arrest and family services had appeared to take Lottie away.

"I'm totally fine, honey."

"That's what Zack said. That you'd be getting a cast and I could draw hearts on it to help your arm get better faster."

The man never failed to astound her. What a great way to reassure a child.

Heather set her sights on him—dark hair disheveled, his winter jacket singed—a knight in shining armor if she'd ever seen one. If he hadn't appeared at her apartment tonight, she might not be sitting here.

"You arrived in the nick of time."

"Not really. You had the situation handled. I put out the fire. That's all."

"That's a lot. How did you know where to find me?"

"I asked Ruth for your address. Said you'd left a few of Lottie's things at my place, and that I wanted to return them."

Normally, she had a terrific memory. Tonight, with the clunk on her head, she was a few steps behind. "What did I leave?"

"Nothing. I just had to see you. Didn't like how we parted."

That made two of them. But, instead of discussing it, he went on with his original story.

"When the fire alarm went off and people started coming out of the building, I went in," he explained. "I heard the commotion behind your door and smelled the smoke. So I grabbed the fire extinguisher from the hall and...you know the rest."

Zack helped Lottie up on the bed beside her, while his tale spun around the wool clogging Heather's brain. "I can't believe Doug was at the center of all this."

"Do you know how he's doing? I asked the nurses, but I'm not family, so they wouldn't tell me anything."

"The burns aren't serious, but he'll be black and blue for a while."

"Serves him right. Turns out he's the one who bribed Connor Trivett. Showed him several photos of you, so he'd know who to identify."

Poor Fern. Her obsession with having a baby must have driven Doug to desperation. To the point where he felt he had to take another woman's child. Heather hadn't imagined how much they'd suffered as a couple.

"My sister became really attached to Lottie when she helped me out last year. I should have invited her to visit more often."

"I don't blame you for steering clear of her husband. The man's got serious problems. We had quite the conversation. Took me for his savior once I handed him an icepack for his groin. He told me the news footage of the fire gave him the idea to frame you. Figured if he could get you behind bars, along with Chase, family services would award Fern permanent custody of your daughter."

A cruel plan. Didn't he have any sympathy for his niece?

"What about my hoop earring? Did he take it?"

"Claims he found it when you were staying with them. Kept it from you out of resentment, because he knew how much you loved the set. He gave it to Connor, along with the photos and a description of your car...to use as evidence against you."

Heather closed her eyes, recalling the moment she recognized Doug as her intruder. "Lottie never liked that guy. Me neither, actually. I'm going to start trusting my instincts."

"She likes me," Zack said with a grin.

Though Lottie had every reason to fear a man after tonight's ordeal, she didn't shy away from Zack. Not anymore. He handed her a set of colored markers and she set to work, decorating the cast.

"She's an excellent judge of character," Heather agreed.

"We saw Auntie Fern in the waiting room, Mommy."

"She wants to see you," Zack informed her. "Wants to apologize for what her husband put you through."

"There's no need." Fern had always been there for her, ready to help, or lend a shoulder to cry upon. Heather would do the same for her sister.

"She mentioned your parents called. They want to talk to you, too."

Heather wasn't quite ready for that. Not with her head fuzzy and her heart confused. Maybe they'd get to the point where they could heal as a family, but she wasn't going to get her hopes up.

"Zack said we'd all be going home to Carol Falls. Is that right, Mommy?"

Heather looked at the man in question, squinting as a blade of light from the fluorescents pierced her skull. "Home?"

"You're free to leave the hospital," he said. "But you've got a concussion. You'll need someone to look after you."

"Are you volunteering for the job?"

"If you'll let me."

Let him? Was this the same Zack Jones she used to know? The one determined to help, whether she wanted it or not?

In this case, with her brain concussed, she definitely needed it. And Zack was her number one guy to lean on. She'd bet he'd earned all his Boy Scout badges as a kid.

"Well...I will need a driver for a day or two. I received a phone call right before you came in. From Garret Frost. With the charges against Peter Boychuk, Sylvia suggested someone go through the farm's books for the last few years to make sure everything's in order. She recommended me."

Zack didn't look surprised. "I think my mom put in a good word for you."

"Juliette, too. If everything goes well, Frost Farms will sponsor me to upgrade my bookkeeping skills. Garret hinted I could end up with a permanent, full-time job."

"That's terrific."

"Mommy, I'm so proud of you."

Heather sniffed back a tear. When was the last time anyone told her that?

"Don't hold in those tears on my account," Zack said,

smoothing her hair. "Sometimes, you just need to let them flow."

Her mouth opened in amazement. Tears rolled down her face. "Who are you? And what have you done with Zack Jones?"

"Would you believe me, if I told you he never existed?" He kissed her bandaged forehead. "I'll share the whole story with you when you're feeling better. For now, all you need to know is that I learned a lot today. With the help of my mother, and Sylvia Frost."

Heather mopped her wet cheeks with the sleeve of her hospital gown. "Coincidentally, we're invited to the Frosts' for Christmas dinner. Apparently, Duncan has a crush on my little girl."

"He wants me to come over and play with him and SpongeBob," Lottie confirmed. "Duncan's taught him to roll over."

"You're to come too," Heather told Zack, extending the invitation. "Ian thought you might be alone this Christmas."

"Not ever again, if I have my way. Which brings me to *my* good news. Ian announced he's received the funding to hire a deputy chief at the fire hall. Thinks I'll be a shoo-in. As long as I'm willing to shuffle papers."

"If you shuffle papers half as well as you shuffle magic cards, you'll have no trouble at all." Heather rolled her shoulders, the month's tension slowly leaving her body. "It appears everything is leading us back to Carol Falls."

"And you know you've got a place to live."

She didn't want to misread his words. "What are you suggesting, Zack? Are you looking for a roommate?"

"No. A *life* mate. I want a strong, independent woman who can take care of herself. A partner. In everything. I want *you*."

His words sent a thrill through her. His sweet kiss bestowed a second wave of pleasure.

"I come as a package deal," she said, giving Lottie a squeeze.

"When I said *you,* I meant both of you." The corners of his eyes crinkled as he gazed at Lottie.

Her little girl had made great strides, but what about Zack? Would he be willing to father another man's child for the rest of his life? "What do you think, Lottie?"

"I like him. He showed me his card tricks and then we played Go Fish."

"For hours," Zack added.

He reached for Heather's hand. Accepting his felt as right as snow in December. "I love you, Heather. Lottie, too. I've been a fool not to tell you sooner."

"That works out beautifully, Zack. Because I love you, too."

As they kissed again, slow and deep, Heather remembered that old adage...and supported it wholeheartedly. *Honesty is the best policy.*

Then Zack pulled away, his brows bunching. "There's only one thing that might be a problem. Tomorrow night is Christmas Eve."

"And?"

"I'm booked to drive the fire truck around Carol Falls."

"All lit up?"

"That's right. I was hoping this year, I'd have my two special girls with me. You and Lottie."

"Can we, Mommy? Can we, please?" The gleam in Lottie's eyes matched the excitement in her voice.

How could Heather refuse her two favorite people? "You, sir...have got yourself a date."

The following night, the three of them rode the fire truck through the quaint streets of Carol Falls. Zack let Lottie play with the siren, but only a few times. Even with Tylenol, Heather's head could do without the extra noise.

At the end of the evening, Zack carried a tired Lottie into the house, her blond head resting on his big shoulder. When they tucked her in bed, the sleepy little girl remarked, "Mommy...I think we need a baby."

"We do?" Heather glanced at Zack. She stifled a giggle at his wide-eyed surprise. He'd soon learn that old TV personality, Art Linkletter, was right. Kids did, indeed, say the *darndest* things.

"Why do we need a baby, honey?"

Lottie yawned again, before replying. "Because I wanna be a big sister."

Zack's arm curled around Heather's waist. He didn't hold her too tight, didn't hem her in, or crowd her. He held her just right. Supporting her as only he could.

"A baby is something we can definitely work on," he promised them both.

Then he kissed the woman he'd waited for all year. Kissed her right through till Christmas morning.

DEAR READER,

Thank you for joining this journey with Heather, Zack and me. If you enjoyed reading THE GREATEST GIFT, please consider leaving a review.

It's always a pleasure for me to return to the world of Carol Falls. If you'd like to spend more time with the Frost Family and their friends, you can view all the books in the series at

http://www.roxyboroughs.com/books/

And, if you want to stay in touch with me, and find out about my village life in the Canadian Rockies, please visit my website at http://www.roxyboroughs.com/, where you can also sign up for my newsletter.

All the best to you,
Roxy.

Made in the USA
Charleston, SC
06 December 2015